RIDING ON THE WIND

RIDING ON THE WIND

BRIX McDONALD

Avenue Publishing 1st edition December
1997.Copyright © 1997 by Brix McDonald
Avenue Publishing
8205 Santa Monica Blvd. #1140
West Hollywood, CA 90046

Printed and bound in the United States of
America
10 9 8 7 6 5 4 3 2

Library of Congress Catalog Card Number:
97-77039

ISBN 0-9661306-0-X

Cover Art by Lee Sampson ©1997

Acknowledgements

I would like to express my appreciation for and gratitude to all those friends and relatives who read this book as it was progressing and gave me encouragement, praise, tips and pointed out the obvious and stray mistakes. Some of those good people are: Annella Faye, Ramona Gergle, Jack Barnard, Candy Tracy, Jeanne Renner, Marilyn Messa, Jaiom Burger, Stephen Wacker, Barbara Carroll, Vicki and Rebecca Manley, Leslie Rogalski, Kendra Marcus of The Bookstop Agency, and Mary Aymar, who was there at the beginning and, like *me*, wanted to be Carrie Sutton.

I would especially like to acknowledge the contribution of Nancy Jennings who painstakingly edited the original manuscript, thus turning it into somthing readable. And my dear friend Barbara Nelson who did the final copy editing and did it so well.

Finally thanks to my patient and long suffering husband, John McDonald, who supported my writing this book and so lovingly and stubbornly held the vision.

Johnny, this is for you.

1860
The Dream

❧

One

Carrie Sutton could barely sit still on the hard wagon seat. Never in her fifteen years of life had a seat felt so rough or had a trip into town taken so long.

"If you're going to keep dancing around on the seat like some Indian praying for rain, why don't you get down and walk like one?"

Carrie turned to the old man seated beside her and smiled. Hank always tried to sound so gruff but he couldn't fool her, not after all these years. She and her Pa had met Hank in a gold mining camp up in the Black Hills ten years ago when she was just a muddy-faced little girl dressed like a boy. Now the mud was gone— most of the time— from Carrie's face and her Pa was gone from their lives, but she still dressed in boys' clothes and Hank, good ole Hank, was still with her.

"A real Indian wouldn't have to walk," she said. "A real Indian would have his faithful pony to ride. If I had my own horse, a horse like Outlaw, I'd never ride in a wagon again."

"You would pick the most contrary of the Express

ponies to hanker after."

"Maybe that's because I'm so contrary myself," Carrie replied. "And besides, isn't he the most magnificent stallion you've ever seen? I'll never hanker after another horse now that I have Outlaw."

Hank looked at Carrie sideways. "He's not your horse, don't forget that."

"Maybe I could buy him from the Pony Express." He was the only horse she wanted. Just the thought of Outlaw made her smile. He was as shiny black as the feathers on a crow, with a crooked white blaze that ran from his forehead to his nose and four white stockings that stood out handsomely against his blackness. His neck arched proudly and his long tail swished as he pranced around the corral. The best thing about him was his spirit. He was like her, Carrie thought, a maverick, with a fiercely independent streak that made him deserve his name and that got him into trouble with the Express attendants the same as hers got her into trouble almost daily with her stepmother. Outlaw could no more be tamed than she could and she loved him for that. He was more than a mere mount, he was a noble steed. She wanted him for herself; to own him and ride him freely was her only desire. Every time she looked at him she was thankful that their ranch happened to be in the perfect place to be a Pony Express relay station.

"And just how do you intend to buy that horse, huh?" Hank asked. "I sure didn't know you were so rich."

"I was thinking I'd get a job and save up my money."

"Is that right? What kind of job were you thinking of?"

Carrie could see the corners of the old man's mouth twitching.

"I thought I might be a Pony Express rider," she said, flicking her long braids over her shoulders and lifting her chin. "After all, I'm fifteen and a half, not what you could call a kid. My own mother, as Pa used to always tell me, was only seventeen when they got married. Cal told me Pony riders make a real good wage. Twenty-five dollars a week! I could buy Outlaw in no time and help out with the ranch, too."

"And what did Cal say when you told him you wanted to be a rider?"

"I didn't tell him. Or Jack. I wanted to tell you first. I thought you'd probably understand better than anyone else. Don't you think I'd be a good Pony rider? I ride and shoot better than most boys, you've said it yourself a hundred times."

The look on Hank's face stopped her. It was the same look he'd worn when she'd been ten and had decided she must become an Indian scout after one had passed through the mining camp, or the time when her Pa had announced that he was going to buy land and become a rancher or, most recently, just two years ago, when Pa had made up his mind to marry Anna. It was a doubting look that struggled against the love and loyalty in his heart.

"I mean it this time, Hank, I really do. I'm not a child anymore, changing dreams all the time. I'm practically grown-up."

Hank shook his head. "But you're still dreaming."

Maybe she was dreaming but she could try, couldn't she? She gazed out over the quiet land of new spring grass, dark green shrubbery and low rocky hills. Behind wispy clouds the sky was blue and clear, freshly washed by the recent rain. It was the country her father had loved, the country where he had begun to turn his dream into reality. He would have made it, too, if he had lived. Wherever he was now, Carrie had the feeling that he was watching her, believing in her. He'd always said anything was possible and he'd never lied.

It was a morning in early spring and the weak sun, doing its best to dry the earth after days of rain, seemed to hold a promise of warmer days to come. After a typically long, cold Wyoming winter, even a hint of warmth was a welcome relief. All the misery of the past year seemed to evaporate. Who could be unhappy on a day like this?

It was, Carrie thought, the perfect day for the start of the Pony Express.

They arrived in Box Elder at midday, riding into a town enthralled by the excitement of the Pony Express.

Box Elder, a fairly new settlement on the western frontier, was cradled in a valley surrounded by foothills that led to the Laramie mountain range beyond. It was a town of ranchers, farmers, fur trappers, miners and emigrants who had stopped to rest themselves and their animals before pressing on westward. Wagon trains of all sizes camping outside of town were a common sight; the horses tethered to the backs of their covered wagons; the cattle, and sometimes sheep, kept in tight circles by tired, dirty cowboys; the women taking care of domestic chores like the laundry that hung across ropes strung between the wagons. Carrie thought they all had faraway looks in their eyes, eyes that were looking at land that was as strange and wild as they'd ever seen, knowing they still had many more dangerous miles to go. For Carrie the wagon trains and their inhabitants had been the only interesting things about the town. Until now, until the Pony Express.

Now Box Elder was part of the Pony Express route. Six

fine Express ponies shared the town livery with miners' mules and farmers' plow horses, and a room at the hotel had been set aside to serve as a home station for two Pony riders.

On this particular day, the third of April—the day the first Pony rider was setting out from St. Joseph, Missouri— although the mail wouldn't reach them for another three days, there was a sense of festivity and anticipation throughout Box Elder, evident in the banner that had been strung across the face of the hotel: "WELCOME PONY EXPRESS!" Murphy's Saloon was doing a booming business and caught Carrie's attention as the wagon rolled into town and made its way down the muddy road to the Mercantile.

"Hey, Hank, what do you suppose is going on over there?"

She stretched her neck for a better look.

"Prob'ly something to do with the danged Pony Express." Hank looked at Carrie. "Whatever it is, you'd best stay away from there."

Carrie laughed and jumped from the wagon. "I was just wondering is all."

"Now, missy, I see that look in those wicked brown eyes of yours and I'm warning you, stay away from there. That's no place for a girl."

"You know I'm not much on warnings," she teased.

"Well, I can't stand and argue with you when I've got supplies to load so's we can get on home before dark." Hank glared at her through bushy brows. "I won't say this again, but you know you shouldn't be going anywhere near a saloon."

Carrie had to suppress a smile at what she thought of as Hank's "stern face". I suppose I'm old enough to know what I should and shouldn't do."

Hank shook his head and disappeared into the dim interior of the Mercantile.

Carrie stared down the road at the saloon. Every time the doors swung open, there was a burst of piano music and loud voices. Men were going in and coming out and the ones coming out were singing boisterously, laughing or stumbling. She recognized some; there was Riley Jones, the livery owner, on his way in, and old man Turner, who was usually so glum, coming out swaying on his feet and looking downright cheerful. There was more than the usual drinking and card playing going on in there, and Carrie guessed that probably one or two of the Pony riders were being entertained.

I'm going in there and nobody's going to stop me, she

thought. It's not my fault I'm a girl. What Hank doesn't know, or what he only thinks he knows, can't hurt him, can it? Or me. She headed for the saloon with an air of casualness, tucking her long braids up under her hat and pulling the brim down over her eyes. Now she could pass for any other boy on the street.

I'll just act like I'm looking for someone, she thought, and I'll slip in and stand in the back. Her heart began to beat a little faster in anticipation.

The sound of boot heels clomping along the boardwalk behind her made her hunch her shoulders forward and lower her head. At any moment she expected Hank's gnarled old hand to come down upon her shoulder. She let herself relax a little, knowing that whoever was coming was walking too fast to be Hank. A tall man, dressed all in black, strode past her. She recognized him immediately. Captain Joe Slade always wore black and wore his gun belt low on his hips, the fancy pearl handles of his pistols showing above their holsters.

Slade was the Pony Express division agent from Fort Laramie. He supervised the relay stations from Fort Laramie to Sweetwater, one of which was the Sutton relay. When Slade had first started riding out to their ranch in preparation for the Pony Express, Hank had warned her to steer clear of him. "That ole Slade has a bad reputation. It's said he's responsible for the deaths of twenty-six men. Maybe more. He came out here to the west after killing a man in cold blood in Illinois."

His presence always gave Carrie the willies. He made her think of a snake in the grass, a poisonous snake but without the warning of a rattle.

"Why would the Pony Express hire a man like that?" she had asked Hank.

"Well, I reckon because they know, as anyone who knows the land along the Overland routes do, that from Fort Kearney, Nebraska to Carson City, Nevada there's no law and order to speak of. The Pony Express is going to have to be that law over most of its course. They'll need people like Slade, as hard and ruthless as he is, to take control over the most lawless areas."

Well, he might be perfect for the job but that didn't mean Carrie had to like him and she didn't. She hated the way he sneered at everyone, and she hated his manner in giving orders. She'd seen enough of him out at their ranch in the last few months; she did not want to meet up with him here in town.

Carrie watched as he came to the end of the walkway and stepped down onto the muddy ground. She thought he would cross the street and go on, but he surprised her by first looking around furtively and then slipping to the side of the building. She ought to go on into the saloon, while she had the chance, but she couldn't, not yet. What was Slade doing sneaking around behind the Mercantile?

Around the corner of the building was a pile of crates and she eased herself behind them, peeking out to see where Slade had gone, feeling like the Indian scout she'd once wanted to be.

There were two other men with Slade and they were strangers. They were dressed like dandies in tailored suits and wide-brimmed white hats and looked as out of place as peacocks would in the frontier environment. She couldn't hear what they were whispering. What *was* Slade doing? Maybe he was just meeting a couple of friends... behind the Mercantile? That couldn't be. Besides, it was common knowledge that Slade had no friends. He was up to no good, Carrie thought.

The shorter of the two fancy fellas held a gun and kept looking over his shoulder nervously. The taller one seemed more at ease, laughing and slapping Slade on the back in a familiar manner. Slade wasn't laughing or acting nervous. He stood before the men coldly, listening to the tall one talk. After a few moments Slade picked up a twig and drew lines in the dirt at their feet while the others watched intensely.

Finally they shook hands, nodding to one another. The two strangers went off towards a small grove of trees where a couple of horses were tied and waiting. Slade paused long enough to wipe his boot over what he'd drawn in the dirt, then started back to the front of the building. Carrie shrank back behind the crates and held her breath. He walked passed her without a glance and she let her breath out in a whoosh of relief.

He went around to the front of the building, stepped onto the boardwalk and sauntered off as though he didn't have a care in the world. He looked downright self-satisfied, Carrie thought, as she fell into step a few yards behind him. She wondered what his reaction would be if he knew she'd witnessed his secret meeting. Carrie shivered. He'd probably kill her in an instant, like he had that man in Illinois.

Slade passed through the swinging doors of the saloon and Carrie was suddenly reminded of her original quest and the limited time in which she had to accomplish it. Slade was forgotten in an instant, pushed to the back of her mind to be examined later.

The saloon and its festivities beckoned her.

Two

Carrie paused outside the saloon long enough to adjust her hat, making sure her braids were coiled securely beneath it. Then acting more casual than she felt, she swung the doors open and stepped inside.

Cigar smoke drifted lazily toward the ceiling and hung there in great, gray clouds. A strong smell of whiskey permeated every corner of the dark, dank room and competed with the odor of unwashed men and cheap perfume. The place was packed with men and boys of every description. Here and there "fancy" women who, except for the occasional angry and unstoppable wife, were the only type of female allowed inside, circulated among the men. A piano player was thumping out a lively tune in the background which no one seemed to be listening to. And Carrie quickly saw why. A young man stood on the bar talking loudly, a bottle in one hand, his hat in the other. As he talked he gestured with one or the other.

Carrie's eyes widened at the sight of him. He was dressed in a spotless fringed buckskin suit and shiny new boots. There was not so much as a speck of dirt on him. He had an angular, high-cheekboned face with a smile that lit his face and beamed on all the faces staring up at him in fascination. His shoulder-length, blond hair seemed to form a halo around his head, and his voice, rich and resonant, was not a bit slurred from drink, although he drank generously from his bottle every few minutes.

Except for her Pa, Carrie had never seen a handsomer man than this tall, self-confident youth who held the occupants of the saloon so enthralled.

He was saying, "And I realized then and there that mining weren't for me, no sir. I'm in my nineteenth year and I possess a big ole appetite for adventure. Well, folks, I found it. Yep, I found it with the misters Majors, Russell and Waddell and their new Overland Pony Express!"

His audience cheered loudly and somewhat drunkenly and the man in buckskin took a generous swig from his bottle.

"I weren't exactly sure they'd have me at first," he continued.

"They looked me over real careful like. They have to, they've got to have the best ponies and the toughest, most experienced men to ride 'em. And that's me, folks, William F. Cody!"

The crowd cheered again with enthusiasm. Carrie pushed her way through the crush surrounding Cody, forgetting her plan to stay in the back unobserved, until she stood directly in front of him. She felt that her heart would beat right out of her chest.

"You all can call me Billy, same as all my friends do!" Cody shouted over the din.

"Hey there, Billy," someone called from the crowd. "We've heard that you're supposed to be some kind of buffalo hunter. I've heard you called Buffalo Bill. What'd you ever do that was so great?"

Cody took a long swig from the bottle, sat himself on the edge of the bar and looked around the room for a moment. His eyes met Carrie's and he smiled.

He knows I'm a girl, Carrie thought, panicked.

"I'll leave it up to this young fella," Cody said, nodding at Carrie. "Well, boy, you want to hear what I done one time when I was out hunting buffalo with some army fellas?"

Carrie, relieved, nodded. It was all the encouragement Cody needed.

"I was out hunting, like I said, with some older fellas, army scouts is what they were. Well, sir, I took down four buffalo right out of the herd without spooking any of the other buffalo and afore any of those scouts took even one. Shoot, they could have just gone behind me and picked up the carcasses. The way I done it, so quiet, none of them even knew any of the herd had been killed. And that was when I was a mere boy of sixteen!" He paused and looked around at the astonished faces of the crowd. Carrie had to ask, "How'd you do that?"

"I done it with a bow and arrows." Cody said.

"A bow and arrows!" Carrie forgot that Slade was somewhere in the room and that he knew her voice, or that there were others who might recognize her voice, forgot everything in wanting to keep this beautiful stranger's attention focused on her.

"Yup. I know me a few tricks and one of 'em is an Injun hunting trick. What I done was rub some buffalo chips on my jacket and on my horse. To disguise my smell, see? If a buffalo can't smell you, shoot, he won't take no notice of you at all."

"That story stinks worse than any buffalo chip I ever smelled." The silky smooth voice came from behind Carrie. Too late she realized that she had completely forgotten Slade's presence in the room and now he stood inches away. She could almost feel his breath on her neck. She hunched forward and pulled her hat down in an effort to remain, she hoped, anonymous.

Cody laughed. "Hey, here's Captain Joe Slade, our

esteemed Division Agent. What are you doing so far from Fort Laramie, Captain?"

"Tying up loose ends for the Express and making sure my riders are getting to their home stations. I don't seem to recall the Express assigning you to this saloon."

Carrie sneaked a look and saw Slade's eyes narrow as he glared at Cody. Maybe he hadn't identified her voice after all. She would have to get out of there as quick as possible.

Cody was not going to be easily intimidated and he replied lightly. "Now, Captain, I heard you ain't opposed to lifting a glass or two yourself."

There were sounds of agreement from the crowd. They were probably hoping a fight was brewing, an entertainment they'd appreciate every bit as much as listening to Cody brag and tell stories.

Carrie felt like a trapped animal. She kept her head down and her back to Slade while looking for a way through the crowd to the door.

"You took an oath, Billy, remember?" Slade said snidely.

Cody tapped his fingers against his forehead. "Let me see now. Yep, I reckon I do remember."

"And I believe there's something in that oath about drinking intoxicating liquors."

"That's right, Captain, and that's some memory you've got." Cody said. "I believe it also says that I will not use profane language or quarrel or fight with any other employee of the Pony Express. So help me God."

"Very nice, Billy. Tell me, are you determined to disgrace the Pony Express so early in the game?"

Cody sat on the bar and contemplated Slade. He set his bottle down deliberately.

"Just what are you trying to do, Captain, provoke me into breaking another of them rules?"

Slade tensed. "Are you threatening me with violence?"

"No." Cody paused. "With profane language." And he burst into laughter.

The crowd roared along with him and the tension, in all but Slade, was eased. Cody managed to stop laughing long enough to say gaily, "Could be I ain't drinking an intoxicating liquor." He picked up his bottle and waved it in the air. "It's just sarsaparilla? Ask the barkeep."

A fresh wave of laughter swept the crowd and they applauded and cheered. Carrie could almost feel Slade flushing with impotent rage. His hand came down on her shoulder and he squeezed it so hard she flinched.

Slade spoke loudly to be heard over the uproar. "Do you also encourage little girls to frequent saloons, Billy?"

Carrie tried wriggling out of Slade's grasp but he gripped her even more tightly and with a flourish, pulled her hat from her head.

"Well, sell my horse and buy me a cow, it *is* a girl!" Cody exclaimed.

"Let me go!" Carrie cried as she struggled to pull away. Cody grinned and cautioned, "Better let her go, Captain, she looks dangerous. Could be she bites."

Slade released Carrie abruptly. She lost her balance and fell backward. Cody reached out quickly and steadied her before she could fall.

"Whoa," he said. "Are you all right, little lady?"

Slade spoke contemptuously, "By no stretch of the imagination can this dirty little creature be called a 'lady'."

Carrie straightened herself up and stuck her chin out defiantly. "So who wants to be a lady, anyway?"

"Obviously not you, that's for certain," Slade said. "Now don't make me drag you out of here, Miss Sutton. Come on now."

Cody took Carrie's hand and held it for a moment. "Wait a minute. Is that your name, Sutton? What's the rest of it?"

Carrie was overcome by the sudden sensation of his hand on hers and was surprised she still had the power to speak. "Uh, Carrie Sutton." She found the courage to add, "We're about twelve miles out of town. We're going to be a relay station."

"That so?" Cody said.

"Where's your run take you?"

"I'll be riding 'tween Red Buttes and Sweetwater."

Carrie said "Oh,"with obvious disappointment. Red Buttes was more than fifty miles east. Slade stood behind her, tapping his foot impatiently, waiting to further humiliate her by escorting her to the door. But she didn't care. She'd never felt like this before, never felt such exhilaration just looking at a face. Could there be another one as perfect as Cody's?

Time stood still and every sensation was agonizing. Under the firm pressure of Slade's hand the wool of her shirt scratched her shoulder. Carrie could taste the smoke and odor in the room. The murmuring and shuffling of the men and the soft, continuous piano playing served as accompaniment to the moment, fixed forever in her mind.

Say something, dummy, she commanded herself, hurry or it'll be too late.

"Mr. Cody, I can ride a horse and shoot a gun as good as any man or boy and I think I could be a real good Pony rider. How do I go about signing up?"

The men nearest her erupted into laughter and turned to

their friends and repeated, with great hilarity, what she had said. Slade smirked and closed his hand around her arm and gave it a yank.

"That's enough now," he said. "You've made a big enough fool of yourself by being in this place. Don't make me drag you out of here after all."

"Hey, hey there, Captain, be gentle," Cody warned. He smiled down on Carrie. "Riding for the Pony's a man's job, Miss Carrie Sutton. I don't think ole Majors, Russell and Waddell would take on a girl rider, even one as pretty as yourself."

Did he think she was pretty? Carrie blushed to her toes. Slade's grip was tightening. "Good bye, Mr. Cody," she said quickly. "Maybe I'll see you again when I join the Express."

Slade jerked on her arm, pinching the skin, but she refused to flinch. The crowd made way for them as Slade pulled her toward the door. Carrie twisted around, trying to get a last look at Cody before being ushered through the swinging doors and into the street. She could here him calling after her, "Call me Billy!"

The doors swung shut behind them and Slade released her, giving her a final shove.

Carrie rubbed her arm. "Ow, you hurt me."

"If you persist in dressing like a boy and trying to act like one, you'd better get used to being treated like one," Slade replied.

"I can take it." Carrie let her arm go and straightened her spine, bringing her chin up and affecting an air of disdain.

Slade brushed imaginary dirt from his black coat and with easy, cold malevolence said, "Oh, really? And how's that refined stepmother of yours going to take the news that you've scandalized yourself in front of half the town?"

"I don't care what she thinks." Carrie almost spit the words. "Wouldn't be the first time anyway."

"You'd best watch how you speak to me." Slade frowned and his eyebrows formed a V over his eyes, giving him a vulture-like look. His gray eyes were merciless and Carrie, for all her bravado, felt a shiver up her back at the look in them.

"Don't forget, Miss Sutton, that in a way you represent the Pony Express. And I am the Express law here. What if I decided that some place other than your ranch would make a more advantageous location for a relay station? I know your stepmother is depending on the extra income to finance a return to the east. What if she didn't have that extra income?"

Carrie's face was flushed. This was the first she'd heard that Anna was planning to go home. But that was good news! What did she care if Anna went back East? Good riddance. But Slade was not going to make her back down. What if he knew that she had seen him behind the Mercantile having his secret meeting? She wanted to tell him just to see the look on his face, but something cautioned her to keep it to herself.

"The Pony Express left St. Joe today and it'll be coming through here the day after tomorrow. It's too late to make changes and I know it as good as you," she said.

"You think you're pretty smart, don't you? Well, I'd just as soon let the Sutton Ranch remain a station and let your stepmother get that extra money. I'll be glad to see you go."

"Me?" Carrie said. "What have I got to do with it?"

A knowing smile spread across Slade's thin face. "Well, you're going, too, little girl, didn't she tell you?"

Three

"Now I know why you were so eager to let the Express use our ranch for a relay station!"

"Carrie, will you please try to calm down so that we can talk sensibly?" Anna's voice was calm, which infuriated Carrie all the more.

"There's nothing to talk about. Pennsylvania's where you belong, not me."

"Just because you insist upon dressing like a boy, it doesn't make you one. I can't leave you here. Your father would have wanted you to go with me."

"How do you know what my father would have wanted? You knew him for one year. I knew him my whole life. He would have wanted me to stay right here and be a rancher like he was." Carrie wanted to burst into frustrated tears, plop down and beat her fists on the floor and scream. But throwing a tantrum would be too childish a thing to do. She knew one thing, Anna couldn't make her go anywhere. Carrie mentally dug her heels in.

"I see that look on your face," Anna said. "But the fact is, I'm your legal guardian and, in spite of the short time I knew your father, I believe he would want to know that I was caring for you. For heavens sake, Carrie, you're only fifteen years old. I know you don't think so, but you need a mother."

"I don't need you for a mother. And I don't need you to look out for me." Carrie's voice rose and wavered; she trembled with fury. How dare she, this woman who had come out of nowhere and taken her father away from her, taken him away for what was to be the last year of his life. What could he have seen in this large, plain woman to love? Whatever it was, it had been darn unfortunate that he'd met Anna and married her so quickly. After that, everything had changed.

Anna seemed to think that Carrie's silence was a sign that she'd given in. "Please understand, Carrie, I don't mean to deprive you of anything by taking you back to Pennsylvania with me. On the contrary, I want you to see what else the world has to offer."

"I saw all of the world that I wanted to see when I was traveling with my Pa, and no place is as pretty or a better place to live than this valley. I'm going to stay here with Hank. I ain't going nowhere, not with you or anyone else." Carrie crossed her arms and lifted her chin, a habit that never failed to madden Anna.

"You most certainly will." Anna's voice took on that

prissy, schoolmarm tone that Carrie hated. "You are going to go back east with me and you will learn to be a proper young lady."

The argument ended as most of them did— with their voices raised and Carrie slamming out of the house.

Slogging through the mud on her way to the stable, Carrie made up her mind to run away if she had to, even if it meant being captured by Indians and forced into being a squaw. She shivered at the prospect, but even Indians were preferable to life with Anna in some distant, stuffy city.

Just outside the stable, she ran into Hank and the two newcomers to the ranch— Cal Lindstrom, the Pony Express station attendant, and his assistant, Jack Rising—on their way to the house for supper.

"You didn't have to come looking for us, Carrie," Jack said. "We're on our way. We're never late when there's a meal waiting."

Jack Rising was about the cheeriest person Carrie had ever met. He was young, only a few years older than she was, and he was nice, with wheat-blond hair, sky blue eyes, a lean, hard-looking body, and a wide smile that never seemed to leave his face. The constant smile and good humor mystified Carrie. She wondered how anyone could be so cocky after suffering a bad accident, leaving a pronounced and permanent limp.

"I didn't come to call you in for supper, Jack Rising. It wouldn't matter to me if you came in or not," Carrie said, looking past him at Hank.

Jack put his hand on his chest melodramatically. "Oh, the bitter cruelty of beautiful young women. Here I am, a healthy, if somewhat damaged, gentleman and I can tell by the look in those dark eyes that she prefers the company of a smelly old horse to me."

Carrie looked up at Cal, silently pleading for deliverance from Jack's weak humor. Cal clamped his teeth around the cigar that never left his mouth and placed a bear-like hand on Jack's shoulder. "Jack, sometimes I think you must be blind as well as lame. Can't you see something is troubling the girl? Come along and leave her be." He gave Jack a push toward the house.

"Thank you, Cal," Carrie said. She watched for a moment as they walked away, burly Cal shortening his stride to match Jack's shuffling steps. Then she turned to Hank reluctantly.

"I reckon you had your talk with Miss Anna and it didn't go so good," Hank said.

"I'm not going, Hank, and she can't make me. If you're going to stay here on the ranch, then I'm going to stay with you. She thinks she can just drag me off somewhere and turn me into a 'young lady'. Don't that beat all? Well, I'm not going to Pennsylvania or anywheres else with her. This is my ranch, too, and I'm staying right here."

"Maybe you should think on it a bit," Hank said.

"What? But, Hank..."

Hank raised a hand as if to physically stop her flow of words. "Jus' think on it. It ain't going to happen tomorrow, is it? You've got a year or more to figger it out. You're not a little girl anymore and she's got a lot to offer you."

Carrie's eyes began to burn as tears welled up. "You're all the family I've got Hank. She's not family, she's nothing to me. I wish Pa had never met her. I wish she'd just go away."

"She ain't really so God awful terrible. You know she allowed as this place was really more mine than hers and she won't be selling it. And she said that when you're all grown up, if you want to come back here, she wouldn't try to stop you. She just wants what's best for you, same as me."

"Nobody knows what's best for me but me!" Tears ran down her face. "My Pa didn't bring me up to be a silly, simpering girl with nothing better to do but read poetry and embroider hankies. I'd have thought you, of all people, would understand. I'd have thought you'd want me to stay!" Carrie turned abruptly and ran to the stables.

The stables were dark and warm with the heat of the horses' bodies. Carrie groped her way to the third stall on the right, Outlaw's stall, and slipped inside. She leaned her face against the stallion's neck and let herself sob.

She didn't know what to do. During the past couple of years her life had been turned upside down. First her father, widowed and happily single all these years, had met Anna Eisenhart, one of a group of schoolteachers who had volunteered to come west to establish schools, and he had fallen instantly in love with her. He hadn't asked for Carrie's permission or approval; his love for Anna had blinded him to his daughter for the first time in her life.

Carrie had been going on fourteen at the time and all of a sudden she didn't know herself, she was changing. Involuntarily her body was growing and shifting. It seemed that one day she was going about her life, with her Pa and Hank, and having a good time, dirty-faced and boyish, and the next thing she knew she had breasts and hips and a stepmother who was appalled by the clothes she wore and kept wanting to make a lady of her.

"Oh, Outlaw," Carrie sniffed. "I know Hank loves me. Why would he side with her against me? She probably talked him into it somehow, convinced him that she was doing what was 'best' for me. She's a mean old thing and I hate her. I'll never go anywhere with her, never. I'll have to make my own way.

"If I got on the Express as one of the Pony riders, there's nothing that she could do to make me leave. I'll be independent then. It'll make Hank so proud he'll want me to stay no matter what she says to try and change his mind. And Bill Cody will hear of me and he won't think of me as some silly little girl.

"I'll be an equal".

Four

The first Express rider came through on schedule the evening of April sixth. The weather had remained unusually clear and though a brisk, chill wind blew across the valley, the sky was cloudless, dotted with stars and accented by a thin sliver of crescent moon.

Cal had selected a dapple-gray mare for this first run; she was lean and sturdy with a swift, sure-footed gait and she was the most manageable of the lot which would be important to the rider, racing over unfamiliar trails in the dark.

Carrie and Hank stood on the road, waiting to hear the sound of the horn that would signal the rider's approach.

"Do you think I'm a good rider, Hank?" Carrie asked.

"Yep," he replied.

"As good as any boy?"

"Better'n most."

"I'm a good shot, too, ain't I?"

Hank looked at her and raised an eyebrow. "Don't start up again."

"I have to be a Pony Express rider. I could do it, Hank, and you know it." The idea of it excited Carrie more and more every time she thought about it.

Hank furrowed his brow, but Carrie could see he was trying to suppress a grin.

"And how do you aim to do that?" he asked.

"I don't know," Carrie said. "But I will, just wait and see. I know you think I'm a fool, but don't you see, after I become a Pony rider and I'm earning my own money, then I can live anywhere and with—or without— anyone I want.

"That you could, I suppose," Hank agreed. "But, you know, it ain't going to be so easy to get on the Express. Do you plan to just sashay on up to ole Joe Slade and say, 'cuse me, Captain Slade, sir, here I am. Sign me on to ride for the Pony.'?"

Carrie shook her head. "I don't guess I can do that."

"He's the one you'll have to ask."

"I know." Carrie grimaced, "He don't like me much."

Hank laughed. "Don't let that stop you. He don't think much of anybody."

"So you think I should try? I could apply direct to those fellas in St. Joe, Mr. Russell or Mr. Majors. I could do that, couldn't I?"

"Well, I don't know, but don't go getting your hopes up," Hank replied.

"But you do think I could do it, don't you? Just think,

Hank, I'll probably think I'm flying, my horse will be going so fast. Imagine that, flying over the mountains and prairies. I'll be the fastest rider they've ever seen, 'cept for Bill Cody, of course. But I'll be just like him and people will gather around me wherever I go and I'll tell them all the stories of my adventures on the trail." She paused to take a breath and felt her heart hammering in her chest. It could happen. She could make it happen.

A cough came from the darkness behind her. Carrie whirled around. "Jack Rising, I know that's you. You'd better not be laughing at me."

Jack, leading the mare, with Cal and Anna following, came up on the road a few feet from Carrie and Hank.

"I'd sooner laugh at a grizzly bear," Jack said.

"Go on and laugh, I don't care. I will be a Pony rider and no one's going to stop me, not any of you and not Captain Slade. Jack threw up his hands in mock terror. "I believe you, I believe you." They all jerked their heads up at the sound of hoofbeats, followed closely by the tinny blare of a horn.

Jack held the mare ready and suddenly, out of the night, a rider appeared, pulling hard to stop his lathered and panting horse. In seconds he had jumped down, snatched the mailbags and thrown them over the gray's saddle, leapt on the mare and with only a brief "Thankee" was off again, thundering away towards the next station.

The months of preparation and anticipation were over in that short minute. The Pony Express was on its way!

That night Carrie had a dream which, with slight variations, would recur for months to come.

She dreamt she was a Pony rider, the wind whipping her hair out behind her, Outlaw's mane slashing against her face as she rode, hunched in the saddle, leaning low over the stallion's neck, urging him on. The staccato sound of the hooves beat out a rhythm that became the beating of drums—Indians on the warpath! She suddenly knew that she was riding into an ambush.

Then Cody was there on the dapple gray and all around him lay dead buffalo. He was holding up a bow and arrow which he flung to the ground when he saw Carrie. Gathering his reins, he said, "No time to lose, we've got to get the mail through. We're going to have to fly." And they did. The horses glided smoothly into the night sky as if it were the most natural thing in the world. They were up among the stars, leaping over a bright, white moon. Below her she could see the Indians massing in confusion. She could see the entire valley and the mountains looming ahead of them. She could see the ranch and tiny figures crossing from the house to the stables. Looking more closely, she saw it was Hank and was that her Pa? It was! Pa was back, he wasn't dead after all!

She called out to Cody, "I have to go back, my Pa's come home!" But Cody reached out and grabbed Outlaw's reins.

"We've got to get the mail through," he said. "Can't stop now." Carrie tried desperately to get the reins back. She stretched forward, her fingertips just brushing them, and she slipped from the saddle and fell and fell.

Carrie woke with a start. There was moisture on her forehead and upper lip, her hands were clammy and her throat was dry. She gulped. It had been a dream. No Cody. No Pa. Throwing the blanket away from her, she crawled to the edge of her bed and pulled herself up to look out her small window. There was the barest twinge of gray in the sky, the slow start of dawn.

Her dream was still with her as she quickly pulled on pants and, with trembling fingers, buttoned her shirt. It had been so vivid: Outlaw's forceful gallop, Cody, rising into the sky and her father's rugged, tan face looking up at her. Dreams were so real sometimes, Carrie thought, they could leave a person with expectations. It was almost as if Pa had come back. She forced the image from her mind.

Her father would not be coming back, couldn't possibly. She had seen his body the day they brought him back, hanging across his saddle, shot and killed for the three dollars he'd had in his pocket. She had watched as his body was lowered into the ground. And the continuing reminder of his absence was the cross-shaped marker on the little knoll above the ranch.

She quietly slipped from the house. She hadn't been to the knoll since the first snowfall of the winter. Carrie felt a renewed ache for her father; an ache, she realized guiltily, she hadn't felt in the past couple of weeks, since the arrival of the men and horses for the Express. Could it be so easy to displace the person you had loved most in the world?

She splashed through the shallowest part of the stream, climbed the knoll and sank to her knees beside the cross. It was already warped and weathered after only one year, and it leaned, tilting to one side, as though admonishing Carrie for her lack of attention. She lovingly righted it, pushing it firmly into the soft earth. Someday she would see that there was a fitting gravestone here, engraved with the words, "Seth Sutton-beloved father."

Carrie squeezed her eyes shut and concentrated, trying to reach out to her Pa. "Pa, I miss you so much and I need you. If you were here now I wouldn't even care about Anna.

You wouldn't laugh at me if I told you I wanted to be a Pony Express rider. You'd be proud of me and you'd help me, I know you would."

"I could help you." The voice came from behind her.

"Jack Rising, what are you doing here?"

"I happened to see you slinking away and I figured this was where you were heading, so I followed you."

He sat himself down on the wet grass next to her and they sat silently for a few minutes as the morning awoke and came alive. The dew, like a thick, moist quilt, wrapped itself around them, and from behind the mountains the sun began its rose-hued ascent. There were rustlings in the woods as the night animals settled in for their daytime sleeping and the day animals began to stir. There was the early, tentative bird song high in the trees and from the ranch came the sound of a rooster crowing. The day had begun.

Jack leaned back on his elbows and sighed. "I like this place."

Carrie nodded. "My Pa used to call this a thinking hill. It's the coolest place on the ranch in summer. I always come up here when the weather's good and just look at the clouds."

"And what were you thinking about this morning, how

to get on the Pony Express?"

"What's it to you?"

"I thought I might help you," Jack said. "You may find this hard to believe, but before my accident, I used to be quite a fancy rider. I even did some trick riding. I think I could teach you a few things that could make you a better rider."

"I already know how to ride better'n most people." Carrie frowned at him.

"I can make you better."

"Why should you?"

"I don't know, maybe because you remind me of my little brothers and I was always helping them." He grinned so hard his eyes squinted.

"You really think you're pretty funny, don't you?"

"No, I think you're funny. Why don't you stop being so stubborn and let a person help you if he wants to? There's not always enough to keep me busy between riders, you know." He smiled at her so sincerely she had to smile back and smiling, she relaxed.

"All right, you can teach me these fancy riding tricks of yours," she said.

"You are too kind to me." Jack clasped his hands to his chest. "Oh thank you, thank you, pretty lady."

"Stop it."

"What? Gratitude makes you uncomfortable? Oh, I get it. Flattery makes you uncomfortable. Well, you are a pretty girl, so you'll just have to learn to live with it."

Carrie shook her head. "The last thing I want to be is a pretty girl. What's that good for? If I were a man, I could go anywhere and do anything I wanted." She paused a moment. "I don't guess there's anything I can do about that so I just have to do the best I can with what I've got."

Jack lowered his eyes to his left leg. "That's all anyone can do."

"Say, Jack, have you or Cal heard any talk in town about Express supplies missing or anything like that?" Carrie asked.

"What do you mean?"

"I saw Joe Slade sneaking around behind the Mercantile the other day in town and I followed him and—"

"What? Haven't you been told not to mess with Slade? He's a dangerous man who—"

"Who's killed too many men to count. I know, I know. Well, he didn't see me, all right? I hid behind some crates and he never knew I was there. Anyway, he met two men. I swear, he was up to something. I've been thinking about it and I thought maybe he was selling Pony Express supplies. Maybe even the horses." The thought made Carrie go cold. What if Slade came out to their ranch on some pretense and took Outlaw away to be sold? Outlaw had to be the most valuable horse the Express had. Carrie could see Jack was interested. He was watching her and frowning, his usually soft blue eyes hardening.

"They were hiding, after all." Carrie concluded.

"You're sure that's what they were doing? The town was in an uproar over the Pony Express, right? Maybe they wanted some quiet place to talk,"

"I'm telling you, Jack, that ole Slade acted like he didn't want to be seen. I wish I could have heard what they were talking about."

"Have you told anyone else about this?" Jack asked.

"No. I wasn't sure if I should. So what do you make of it?"

"I think it's kind of interesting is all. It's certainly nothing to get worked up over."

"Maybe we should report this to someone. Maybe we should tell Cal and see what he thinks."

"No, Carrie, don't do that. Not yet. There's no need to make something out of nothing."

"Nothing? But, Jack— "

"It is nothing. You didn't hear what they were saying.

You don't know what was going on. You can't go making accusations blindly."

"I know what I saw," Carrie said stubbornly.

"Look, I don't have time for intrigue right now. I have horses to feed and tack to clean and stalls to muck out." Jack rose clumsily to his feet. He stood over her and offered his hand. She took it reluctantly and he pulled her up. She was still thinking about Slade. "I'm glad I followed you up here, though," Jack continued, looking around. His glance paused briefly on Seth's grave marker. "This is a nice spot."

"Yeah. You said when you saw me leave you knew I was coming up here. How did you know that?" Carrie brushed grass and twigs from her damp pants.

"I knew your father was buried here. Your mother pointed it out to me one day."

Carrie felt her face go hot. "She is not my mother! My mother died when I was a baby. She's nothing but my stepmother and it wasn't by any choice of mine. I hate her."

"I don't think I've ever hated anybody or anything in my life, not even the horse that lamed me," Jack said, looking at Carrie in wonder. "What did she do to make you hate her?"

"She married my Pa."

"That doesn't seem like reason enough. From what I've seen, she seems like a good woman. I'll bet she loved your Pa and made him happy."

"I don't want to talk about her, all right? So just you leave it alone. It's none of your business anyway." The words came out harsher than she had intended.

Jack shook his head. "You're a hard-hearted girl, Carrie Sutton. It's a terrible thing to have an unforgiving nature like you do." He began to limp stiffly away from her. He stopped at the stream and turned back. He smiled. "I'll still give you those riding lessons."

Carrie watched him move away and an unfamiliar sensation began to grow in her. She realized that, in spite of her harsh words, Jack liked her and was willing to be her friend and, in spite of his constant teasing, she liked him, too. It felt good to have someone near her own age to talk with. It might be nice to have a friend, she thought.

Five

"Stop looking so uncertain; it's not that difficult, Carrie." Jack sounded exasperated. "You grab the pommel with both hands and when the horse starts to pick up speed, you throw yourself up into the saddle. The momentum of the running horse will lift you right up. Understand?"

"Yes, I understand. You've only explained it a hundred times. Your trick just doesn't work, that's all," Carrie said, frustrated.

"This does work, I used to do it all the time. Do you really want to be the best Pony rider in the West or not? If you can get the knack of this, you'll be faster than any of the others at changing horses and mailbag," Jack assured her. "It's up to you."

Carrie could not resist a challenge. "I'll do it."

For the fifteenth time that day she ran alongside Flag, Jack's saddle horse: her left hand clutched the reins and the pommel at the front of the saddle, until the horse broke into a trot, then she gripped the pommel with both hands and, urging him into a canter, pushed herself off the ground. For the first time she felt the lift the way Jack had described it. However there was not enough momentum to lift her high enough. She bellyflopped across the saddle, pulling on the reins as she did, causing the horse to slow. Unable to help herself, Carrie slid head first from the saddle and lay on the ground laughing as Jack limped toward her.

He stood above her and chuckled. "Well, that was pretty close. I think you've got the idea." He helped her to her feet.

"Did it take you this long to learn this?" Carrie asked.

"No, but I had someone showing me, and that probably made it easier than just being told how to do it." Jack said.

"It's hard to believe that you used to do this," Carrie said and instantly regretted the remark. She felt her face grow warm. "I'm sorry, Jack, I didn't..."

"It's all right," he interrupted. "I know it's hard for the people I meet to realize that I wasn't always lame. I used to be the fanciest rider in the county, maybe in the whole state of Kansas. And the reason I got that way was that I practiced and practiced. So, are you ready to try again?"

Throughout the spring months and into the summer Carrie worked at making her riding more skillful. She would entice Jack away from his chores whenever she could, sometimes helping him to finish so he could join her more quickly. Practice was squeezed in between ranch chores, relay station upkeep and the Pony Express riders that came like clockwork twice weekly. As spring turned to summer, Carrie began to think of Jack as a friend.

Her friendship with Jack was a new experience for Carrie. For the first ten years of her life she had led a transient existence traveling with her Pa. After that, they'd settled here on this land and begun building the ranch, thirteen miles and a half day's ride from town. Their nearest neighbors were even farther away. She'd never had an opportunity to develop friendships with anyone close to her own age. She'd never attended a real school; any educating she'd had had come from her father or Hank. Carrie took to reading, writing and doing sums as easily as riding and shooting a gun, but she'd never experienced classroom camaraderie. Until Jack had come along, Carrie had never known she was missing anything.

As time went on, Carrie learned that Jack came from a large, loving family and that they were farmers in Kansas. She also learned that his accident had been caused by his own foolishness in trying to ride a horse that he had been warned was dangerous. He had made his attempt to break the horse early one morning, before anyone else was up. He was certain that he would be the one to tame the untamable. The horse had thrown and trampled him and might have killed him if his younger brothers hadn't chosen that morning to sneak off to go fishing before chores and had been there to intervene.

Carrie told Jack things, too. She found it was fun to share her memories of growing up in the wild west and watch Jack's reactions. Her life had been rather exciting compared to his. There were the years spent in the rough mining camps where, as a little girl, her Pa had started dressing her like a boy for her own safety and there were all the strange and wonderful people they had met in their travels before they had settled here on the ranch. Her adventurous life was a counterpoint to Jack's stable family life. It seemed to Carrie that what each of their lives lacked was what the other had had in abundance. They never ran out of things to talk about.

And Jack never ran out of ways to tease her. The better he got to know her, the more merciless he became, subjecting her to his worst jokes. He would address her by his little brothers' names. Or he'd say, "You think you're so tough, don't you? Come on, let's arm wrestle and see how strong you really are." He would then deliberately lose and he'd cringe and tremble and call her 'Sir'. Or he'd say, "How about a foot race?" and laugh at her discomfort. He would make fun of her or himself, it didn't seem to matter. And she laughed and couldn't stop. There was joy in her life again.

Jack especially liked to tease her about Bill Cody and that was the only joking she didn't find funny. Cody was making quite a name for himself as a Pony rider, but Jack remained unimpressed.

Carrie wanted to talk about Cody. "They're calling him Boss Rider, you know. He's the best rider the Express has got."

"'Boss Rider'. Can you guess who started calling him that? Or I should say, guess who started calling himself that?"

"What? Billy wouldn't do that."

"Oh, right, I've heard he's real humble," Jack snickered.

"If you're going to be mean I guess we just can't talk about Billy." Carrie decided that it must be hard for Jack to hear about the exploits of such an able-bodied man as Cody, when he was stuck with the life of a cripple. Carrie thought Jack would have made a fine Pony rider.

Summer settled on the ranch and with it the worst time of year, harder than the coldest winter months, in Carrie's opinion. She hated the way the grass and brush became brown and lifeless. There was less time for riding practice as the workload became heavier and harder. More water had to be hauled from the well and toted to the stables or

Anna's vegetable garden. Animals and people alike grew lethargic and short-tempered. The only thing that excited Carrie, now that she found the bi-weekly Express riders routine, was her practice sessions and the progress she was making.

It was Hank's idea to make a fake mochila, or saddlebags, like the Pony riders used. The mochila had been invented expressly for the needs of the mail delivery. It was a square leather blanket, with a hard leather mail pocket sewn on each corner. It fitted securely over the saddle horn, but could be removed from one saddle and placed on another in a matter of seconds. Hank made one from leather scraps and surprised Carrie with it in July, on her sixteenth birthday.

"Oh, Hank, this is perfect, what a wonderful idea." Carrie threw her arms around the old man's neck. "You always know the perfect gift to give me." She looked at Anna spitefully. The blue-flowered dress that Anna had given her lay unwanted, draped over the back of a chair. "Now if I could just use a real Express pony in my practicing," she continued, "I'd be the best in no time." She turned pleading eyes on Cal. "Couldn't I use Outlaw for an hour or two a day?"

"No, you can't. That's the best horseflesh money can

buy and nobody's going to wear him out between rides," Cal said firmly, biting into his cigar.

"I wouldn't. I'd just run him back and forth across the yard for a little while. Wouldn't even get him warm. It'd probably be good for him."

Cal frowned. He was a gentle bear of a man but he took his duties seriously. "And, if Captain Slade just decided to ride in to check up on things, unexpected, like I hear tell he does, and he sees you tearing around on one of his good ponies, what do you reckon he's going to do?" The cigar bobbed in his mouth as punctuation.

"Hire me on the spot?" Carrie joked.

"I don't reckon that's likely," Cal replied. "And you oughta quit hanging around with Jack so much, his dumb humor is starting to wear off on you. No, Slade would shoot me right off and then he'd probably fire me to boot. No, sir. So just get it out of your head."

It was no use giving Cal her most crestfallen look. It had always worked when she wanted something from her Pa or Hank, but Cal was not so easily swayed. All the same, she looked at him intensely, disappointment shining in her eyes. To ride Outlaw at least once would be a dream come true.

"How about if you let Carrie ride him for a bit today?"

Jack suggested. "After all, it is her birthday."

Carrie felt a rush of gratitude for Jack, for her good, thoughtful friend Jack. She turned to Cal, hope rising in her. "Say yes, Mr. Lindstrom, please. Only this one time, I promise. Say yes."

"I can't and you know it, and Jack Rising, you should know better than to ask," Cal said.

"My Mama always told me it don't hurt to ask and that I'll never know the answer unless I do," Jack said good naturedly.

"Your Mama was right but my answer's still no." Cal's tone said "and that's final."

Later that day Slade rode in, as unexpected as they'd been warned he could be. Carrie could see the "see, what did I tell you?" as plain as could be on Cal's face. Knowing Cal had been right didn't make her want to ride Outlaw any less and she watched Slade with quiet resentment. He seemed to stand between herself and her dreams.

Slade walked through the stables, giving the station a quick inspection. Later, sitting on the front porch with a glass of cool well water, he told them of the reason for his visit, which wasn't, as Carrie had suspected, to spoil her birthday.

"There's going to be some real trouble with the Indians

here about," Slade said. "Several stations have already been attacked and the stock stolen."

Anna's face paled. "Has anyone been killed?" she asked.

"Well, I don't want to frighten you but, yes, there have been fatalities. But there's nothing to be afraid of now. Colonel Upson has sent a garrison out of Fort Laramie to patrol this entire area. You'll be safe enough."

"You're sure of that, are you?" Anna asked.

Slade grinned. "You need have no fear. We'll wipe out every thievin' Indian between Julesburg and Rock Creek. I have made it clear to my men that to see an Indian is to kill one or answer to me."

"Killing is killing," Anna said. "I don't like it either way."

"That's not the way to deal with the Indians," Jack said.

"I beg your pardon, boy, what did you say?" Slade turned to Jack with a patronizing sneer on his face.

"I said that's not the way to deal with the Indians. They're just fighting for what used to be their land. We white men chase off or kill off their game and we do the same to them, as though they were animals instead of men."

"And what makes you such an expert on Indians?" Slade asked.

"I didn't say that I was. I just know the facts."

"Well, the fact is that valuable stock has been stolen and

some smaller stations have been burned to the ground and men, our men, have been killed. There are hundreds of miles along the route with no defense against ambush or raid."

"Now, sir, if you please," Cal said, "you're going to frighten the womenfolk with that kind of talk. They're liable to forget that we're safe enough here with Captain Upson and his patrol keeping an eye on things. What I'd like to know about is the situation in the South. We don't get much in the way of news out here." The cigar shook in Cal's mouth. "Them Southerners still yammering 'bout States Rights and secession? Is there going to be a war?"

Carrie slumped back in chair and groaned to herself. Once Cal got started on war talk there was no stopping him. She glanced over at Jack and was surprised to see him guardedly studying Slade.

"It's Lincoln who seems to be stirring things up." Slade said.

"You don't care for honest Abe?" Jack asked, acting innocent.

What was he up to? Carrie thought.

Slade sniffed. "'Honest Abe' indeed. Just another politician, if you ask me. They're all alike."

"Now wait a minute," Cal began. Slandering Lincoln was

blasphemy in his book.

"Now, Mr. Lindstrom," Anna said placatingly. "I'm sure Captain Slade didn't mean that Mr. Lincoln wouldn't make a fine president for this country. Did you, Captain?"

"No, of course not." But there was a sneer in his voice.

"Of course not." Jack repeated sarcastically.

Carrie was suddenly alert. She could sense tension in the air. It seemed as if, in some unspoken way, a war had been declared right here on their front porch. The others must have felt it, too. Cal, Hank and Anna seemed to shift uncomfortably in their chairs as they eyed Jack and Slade. The moment passed with a shrug of Slade's shoulders and his abruptly getting to his feet.

"I do have other relay stations to attend to so I'd best be on my way," he said. He turned to Anna. "Remember what I've said regarding the Indians in this area. Be aware but don't be afraid. Captain Upson will be looking out for you."

This was the chance Carrie had been waiting for. She had been finding it hard to contain herself and seized the opportunity. "I'm not afraid, Captain Slade. I'm not scared of anything. I wouldn't be afraid to ride for the Pony. I've been practicing real hard for months now and I could be a darn good Pony rider, if you'd just give me the chance. I'm light, you see, and I have a natural way with horses, don't I, Hank? If you could just watch me, I'd show you how good I am and then you'd see that..."

Slade interrupted, his hand raised. "Wait a minute there, girl. I'm sorry to hear you're still entertaining those ridiculous thoughts and that you've obviously been encouraged to do so. The Express is a hard life: it's no place for a little girl." His smile showed no warmth, only annoyance.

"I'm not a little girl! I turned sixteen today and that makes me fully grown. I'm a good rider. I bet I'm as tough and sharp as any rider you got, 'cept for Bill Cody. Come on, Captain Slade, how about it? Will you take me on?"

The porch, even in the summer heat, seemed to have gotten several degrees cooler.

"Miss Sutton," Slade's voice was like ice. "You are becoming tiresome. I am not in the habit of hiring on young ladies as Pony riders and I do not believe I'll be taking up the habit anytime soon. Is that answer enough for you?"

Carrie was like a terrier with a bone. "Yessir, but I'm not a young lady. My Pa always used to say I was more like a boy than a girl. Didn't he, Hank? So, you see..."

Anna stood up abruptly, taking cups from the men and giving Carrie a meaningful look.

"That's quite enough, Carrie," she said. She turned to Slade. "She's as stubborn as a mule when she gets an idea in her head. She's been Pony Express crazy since this business started. We all have, I guess."

Carrie glared at her, her hands forming fists at her side. Hank put a restraining hand on her arm, but she shook it off and stomped across the porch to stand between Anna and Slade. "She doesn't speak for me. I'm not crazy. I've been practicing since spring and you can ask these men."

Slade stood and picked up his hat. He ignored Carrie, putting his hand out to Anna. "Thank you for the water, Mrs. Sutton. Everything seems to be running smoothly here."

He smiled nastily, looking at Carrie.

"Except some mouths. Again, don't worry about the Indians, but don't let your guard down, either. If the situation worsens, we will send more men out here to help you. I hope you realize that you, and many like you, are doing our country a great service. In these uncertain times, the Pony is a valuable—"

"Don't give me a speech, Captain Slade," Anna broke in, "just keep us safe to do this 'great service'."

Cal walked Slade to his horse, talking all the while.

"Look there, Jack," Carrie said, "Cal's probably arguing my case some more. I bet he could convince Slade to let me ride for the Pony."

Jack snorted, shaking his head. "You've got one track mind and you think everyone else must have too. You might wonder, as I am, why Slade's riding out here alone when there's supposed to be so much danger from the Indians. As for Cal, he's more interested in what's going on in the South and whether it seems likely that Abe Lincoln will win the election. If he does, there probably will be a war, you know."

Carrie gave Jack a look of scorn and stomped off without answering.

Why was everyone suddenly against her, she wondered. She knew there might be a war, she'd heard Cal talk about it often enough and she was willing to do her part by becoming a great Pony rider and delivering important papers and news. So why wouldn't they help her? She wasn't ready to give up, not yet, not ever.

Six

August came and the heat worsened. The creek that flowed down the knoll and behind the house slowed to a trickle, and the grass left on the ground was brown and brittle. Anna had to delve into her moving money to buy additional feed for the cattle and horses. Now, when Carrie and Jack had their practice sessions they wore bandannas around their faces to keep from choking on the thick clouds of dust that swirled up around them.

The heat seemed to make everyone short tempered. Carrie's impatience to be a Pony rider increased in proportion to her growing ability. She could mount a running horse easily and switch horses and mochila in less than a minute; she could shoot while riding and hit any target. She knew she was ready.

"Too bad you're not a boy," Jack said over and over. "The Express would be begging for your help."

Especially now, Carrie thought. The problems with the Indians had gotten worse through the summer and quite a few riders had quit rather than take the chance of ending up scalpless. Some left to be closer to their homes and families in case of war, which seemed imminent as Abe Lincoln's popularity increased. In any case, new riders were in constant demand and Carrie gritted her teeth in frustration. She knew that more and more telegraph poles were being put up. She heard Cal say that when the telegraph was complete, it would make the Express obsolete. She was afraid it would be too late for her.

Carrie longed to see Cody again. She continued to have the same dream almost nightly, of riding alongside Cody as they outran Indians. Sometimes they would flee from telegraph poles. And sometimes in the dream Cody would lean over and kiss her. Carrie would wake from those dreams feeling embarrassed and confused at the intensity that swept through her. *I must be in love with him,* she concluded. She was in love with a man whose face was beginning to fade from her memory. And she had no one to discuss these new feelings with.

She tried to talk to Jack about it.

"Have you ever been in love, Jack?" she asked him, trying to sound merely curious.

He looked at her strangely and hesitated a long time before answering. "Maybe."

"Well, aren't you going to ask me if *I've* ever been in love?" Carrie persisted.

"I don't have to ask, I already know that you imagine yourself in love with the great and noble William F. Cody, who you've met all of once in your whole life."

Carrie could feel pink creeping into her cheeks. "What makes you think that?"

"Well, you mention his name a dozen times a day and when you do, you get this dopey look on your face. Besides, I've heard you baring your heart and soul to Outlaw."

"What!" Carrie's face was aflame. "What are you doing sneaking around and eavesdropping on my private conversations? You're as low as they get, Jack Rising."

"Oh, don't go getting yourself in an uproar. Only you would call talking to a horse a 'conversation.' And I wasn't sneaking around. I just happened to be in the stable when you came in, and I didn't want to embarrass you. But, since you've brought this up, I'm going to tell you straight out that you're an idiot to moon over someone like the glorious Cody. Do you seriously think that he's ever given you a second thought?" Seeing the look on Carrie's face, Jack paused. "I'm sorry to be blunt, but women can be so blind."

Carrie jumped to her feet. "And sometimes men are so stupid! Who do you think you are, Mr Know-It-All Rising? How do you know what Bill Cody thinks? Huh? I thought you were my friend, but I can see there are things we can't discuss. I guess it must be hard on you because Cody is such a man and you're..." Carrie stopped and her hand flew to her mouth. She watched in horror as Jack's face paled.

"I'm sorry, Jack, you know I didn't mean—"

"I know just what you meant, Miss Sutton, and I guess I can't blame you. I don't suppose I'd expect anyone to hero worship a cripple like me."

He got slowly to his feet and limped away.

For the first time in Carrie's life she missed having a mother, a real mother,— Anna didn't count, of course— her own mother who would understand all these confused emotions inside her.

After her disastrous talk with Jack, he became somewhat distant. An ache grew in Carrie, an ache she didn't understand; finally she attributed it to loneliness and missing the easy companionship she'd had with Jack. But she knew it was more than that. Something wasn't quite right and she didn't know what it was or how to fix it.

September arrived but the heat did not lessen; if anything it seemed to increase. There was no relief, not even at night. The vegetables in Anna's garden, which should have been ready for harvesting, were dying. Could it be that the Pony riders were riding more slowly? The horses left by the riders sometimes seemed near death. Carrie worried every time Outlaw was taken out and prayed for his safe return. Outlaw and her constant hope of fulfilling her dream were all that kept her from dissolving into melancholy.

And then the impossible happened. The Pony Express was temporarily discontinued.

A rider came out from town one day and told them what had happened. Several tribes of Indians in Nevada and California had taken to the warpath. For hundreds of miles along the route there was no safety against ambush or attack. The Express, concerned for its riders, had called to the government for help. Alexander Majors declared that he would not allow his riders to risk their lives any longer.

A force was sent out to punish the tribes and restore order along the trail. Major Ormsby, from Carson City, Nevada, was in command. Although he announced that he was "going to get an Indian for breakfast", he knew little about fighting Indians. He and half of his force were killed in a bloody ambush. Those who survived were chased back to Carson City.

It was apparent after this event that the entire mail service was in danger. The Overland Pony Express came to a standstill on the last day of September: no more mails east, no more mails west.

"A good many of the Pony riders and station hands have joined up with the army to fight the Indians," the messenger told them. "They're hoping for a quick end to this dang uprising."

Carrie looked from Cal to Jack. Would they feel that they had to go fight the Indians?

"Well, I reckon all we'll be fighting here is boredom," Cal said, putting Carrie's fears to rest.

Anna was clenching her apron. "Do you think the Indians here in the territories will join in this fight against the white man?" she asked, "We are quite isolated out here."

The messenger shook his head. "No, I think the Indians of this area have been scared off pretty good by Slade and his boys. You'll be all right."

Cal finally allowed Carrie to ride Outlaw. All the Express horses needed more exercise than they got from just being in the pasture, where, in the heat, they only moved if they had to.

The big black and white stallion—who the Pony riders found such a challenge to manage—responded to Carrie as though he were an extension of her, as she knew he would. Hot air blew in her face as they sped across the fields. The troubles with Anna, the falling out with Jack, the impatience to get on the Express, all dropped away in the thrill of the ride. This is living, this is where I'm supposed to be, she thought. I'm going to be the best Pony rider they've ever seen. I've just got to figure out how to make them want me.

One day in late September she ended up on the knoll. She pulled the saddle off Outlaw and rubbed the sweat from him with handfuls of the last of the green grass that grew along the stream. He pushed at her, nuzzling her neck in pleasure, then grazed along the stream, quiet and content. Carrie sat under the shade of the birch trees and spoke aloud, to her Pa, to Outlaw, to herself.

"I guess fall is on its way, after all," she said. The day held a familiar snap of autumn. I can't remember when we've had such a long, hot summer. Does that mean we're in for a hard winter or a mild one? I'll ask Hank; he always says he can predict the weather according to his arthritis." She stretched out her legs and crossed her arms behind her head, gazing at the sky. Under its vast blueness she felt small and lonely. The sky reminded her of Jack's eyes—now wasn't that silly? Still, she wished she hadn't gotten him mad at her, or disappointed with her, or whatever he was. She missed him. She had apologized and he had accepted, but he avoided her nonetheless. She had let her big mouth run away with her and had hurt her best friend.

"So here I am all alone on a beautiful day. I wish I had someone to go riding with. Oh well." She pulled her knees up and hugged them, letting her chin rest on them, and looked out over the ranch. It was getting on in the afternoon; Anna was in the house starting supper, and the men were in the cool of the stable cleaning or fixing tack or just shooting the breeze. The animals seemed less listless, more evidence that the weather was changing. The ranch looked serene and she thought of how much she loved it. A movement towards the back of the house caught her eye.

Someone was creeping up to the henhouse. Then another joined the first. An icy shiver went down Carrie's spine. Indians!

She could see now that there was a small band of them; she counted five, two men and three women. The women were serving as lookouts as the men unlatched and entered the henhouse. The chickens, stupid birds, did not make a single warning cluck. Carrie got to her feet slowly and stayed hidden. She crept to where her saddle lay and picked it up, whistling softly to Outlaw. The sight of Jack, walking up the path, made her jump with fright, then sigh with relief.

"Hey, Carrie," he said. "I was hoping I'd find you up here."

Carrie dropped the saddle and went to Jack in two long strides. "Quiet, Jack. Be still."

"What's the matter? You look like you've seen a ghost." He raised his eyebrows in the direction of her Pa's grave.

She followed his gaze. "Don't be silly. Look." She bent down, pulling Jack with her, and pointed out the Indians. They had captured four fat hens and were leaving the henhouse. "Indians! They're stealing our chickens. What should we do?"

"Nothing," Jack said.

"What? What do you mean, nothing?"

"I mean leave them be. Look."

The men had joined the women and they all turned back to the woods. Two small children were waiting for them; even from the knoll Carrie could see the excitement of the children over the hens. Then they were gone.

"They look like real savages, don't they?" Jack asked her.

"They looked like they were starving." Those children, they were so *thin*.

"They probably were. Slade has forced the Indians in

these parts to hide out. They can no longer hunt to provide for their families. Believe me, they need those chickens more than we do."

"But why does Slade make the Indians out to be such murderers and thieves? Those Indians could have taken horses, too. Or cattle. No one was guarding the stock." It didn't make sense to her.

"I don't know. He's sure trying awful hard to convince everyone and doing a pretty good job of it, too. Which is why the usually honorable Indians are forced to go sneaking around robbing from henhouses." Jack's face was the most serious Carrie had ever seen. "Don't tell the others, all right? If it gets back to Slade, he'll more than likely hunt that band down and kill them. Don't even tell Hank, just to be safe. All right?"

"All right." Carrie picked up her saddle and whistled to Outlaw. "Does this mean you've forgiven me, really forgiven me?"

"I told you before that I did."

"What I mean to ask is, can we be friends again?" Carrie turned her back to throw the saddle over Outlaw's back.

"Yes," Jack said. "But I never did stop being your friend."

"Well, then, I should tell you, I like my friends a little

less silent."

Jack laughed and Carrie smiled at the sound.

They walked back to the ranch, laughing and talking, leading Outlaw between them. Carrie thought it was a day she'd always remember; the perfect Indian summer day — complete with real Indians— her precious friendship with Jack re-established, Outlaw at her side, everything just right.

They were coming into the stable yard when a familiar sight caught Carrie's eyes. "Jack, look, can you believe it? It's Bill Cody!" She laughed and whooped with delight. Jack didn't laugh with her, but she hardly noticed.

Seven

Bill Cody was there, eating supper with them and it wasn't a dream this time, he was truly there.

Cody finished the last scrap and leaned back in his chair. He started to run his sleeve across his mouth, then seeing that Anna was looking at him, used his napkin sheepishly.

"That was mighty good. Mighty good. Thank-you, Miz Sutton. Ain't had a meal like that since my own ma died." His charm was infectious and Anna returned his smile.

"Thank you, Mr. Cody. that's quite a compliment," Anna said.

Carrie had hardly touched a bite of her food. The nearness of Bill Cody, after so many months, was almost making her physically ill.

"So, Mr. Cody," Cal said, "do you have any news about what's going on up North and in the South?"

Carrie groaned silently. Not war talk, not tonight.

"First off, call me Billy— I ain't hardly deserving of no 'Mr.'– and second, yup, I heard that if Ole Abe is elected, South Carolina will surely secede and if she does, others will follow."

"I knew it!" Cal slammed his fist on the table for emphasis. "There's going to be a war as sure as I'm sitting here. Them Southerners don't know what they're getting themselves into."

"Mr. Lindstrom is a fervent abolitionist," Anna explained to Cody.

Cody nodded. "So am I, Ma'am, so am I. I wish they didn't have to make a war over it, though."

"Those damn, uh, sorry ladies, those southerners just won't have it any other way. They buy and trade on human lives as if they were animals. It makes my blood boil." Cal was warming to one of his favorite subjects.

"Does that mean you'll be joining the Union forces?" Cody asked.

"Well, of course, I won't run out on the Pony Express, but as soon as I'm no longer needed in its service, yes, indeed, I will join the fight," Cal replied.

"Do you think the Express is going to survive this Indian uprising?" Carrie asked, glad for an opportunity to change the subject.

"I believe we will be back in the saddle by next week. What's more, we will continue to make deliveries twice weekly." Cody said.

Carrie sat up straighter in her chair. "The Express is going to have to hire on more riders, aren't they?"

"Carrie," Anna's voice held a warning.

Carrie ignored her. She had been wanting to speak to Cody alone and had been making up a speech but since the opportunity was here, she plunged in.

"Mr. Cody-" She began.

"Now, Miss Carrie, didn't I ask you to please call me Billy?"

Carrie blushed roses into her cheeks. "I need your help." It came out as a squeak.

"How's that?"

Carrie tried to make her heart beat slower and she fought an urge to stammer. "I need your help to get onto the Pony Express." Saying the words strengthened her and she was able to look him directly in the eye.

"What?" he said.

"Oh, Carrie," Anna said despairingly.

There was a moment of silence during which Carrie did not remove her eyes from Cody's. Blood was pounding in her head and her hands began to shake. She knew she wouldn't be able to stand up if she tried, but she didn't care. Billy would help her, he had to.

Cody began to laugh, throwing his head back and slapping his knee. Anna smiled hesitantly, as did Cal and Hank. Jack glared at Cody, his muscles tensed, until he glanced at Carrie and saw that she was smiling, too.

"Girl, you're a lot like them Indians, you just don't know how to quit, do you?" Cody said.

"Not when I want something as bad as this."

"That's enough, Carrie," Anna said, "You can play Pony Express, but this is going too far."

The authority in Anna's manner did not intimidate Carrie; it made her more rebellious. She made a point of ignoring Anna and spoke to Cody as though there had been no interruption.

"It may sound foolish, but I'm not. I've been practicing all summer and I'm good. Ask Jack there, he's been helping me. Or ask Hank or Cal. We timed the riders on their exchanges of the mochila and we timed me and I'm faster by half." Carrie turned to Jack for confirmation. He just looked at her. "Tell him, Jack. Tell him how good I am."

Jack remained silent and she looked at him quizzically.

"Yeah, Carrie's real good," he finally said.

Cody turned back to Carrie. "Can you ride hard and fast for thirty miles or more in any weather and do it day after day? I think I could." She squared her shoulders and lifted her chin.

"And how is it you think I could help? I'm just one of the riders" Cody said, as if expecting a protest.

74

Carrie didn't disappoint him. "You're the best rider they got. They call you Boss Rider. I heard some folks call you that when I was in town. If you were to give me a recommendation, write it out and all, that'd lean 'em my way; I know it would."

Cody looked at Carrie with real concern. "Do you think Slade would give you a job on my word? I'll bet he's not one of 'em who calls me Boss Rider. Besides, I haven't even seen you ride. You really think you could hold up to hard riding and a life of danger?"

"I'm tougher than I look," Carrie said.

"Please don't encourage her, Mr. Cody" Anna said.

Cody smiled at Anna. "Miz Sutton, Carrie could prob'ly take my recommending note and one from the President of the United States directly to Mr. Russell and Mr. Majors and Mr. Waddell, and I still don't reckon they'd hire on a girl rider."

Carrie stared at Cody, numbed for a moment. To be grouped thoughtlessly with all girls, for Cody not to see how special she was, was unthinkable.

"Thank you for that," Anna said, "The men humor her and we've all enjoyed seeing Carrie practice and get so skilled, but I'd rather see her suffer a minor disappointment now than to get her hopes up and suffer a greater one later."

Carrie jumped to her feet and faced Anna. She shook with rage. "I never asked for your approval or say so on this or anything, and I'll thank you to keep your prissy nose out of it! You come along and spoil everything all the time! I hate you!" She stomped her foot for emphasis. Tears were threatening to escape to her cheeks and rather than add that to her humiliation, she ran out the door.

The sun was setting, casting its purples and reds over the valley in the spectacular way of mountain lands. There was usually a kind of comfort for Carrie to be found in the beauty of the hour before darkness fell. As one day ended, there was a hope for the new day to follow and a whole night to dream of what that day might bring.

But now, running blindly from the house, there was no comfort now, no beauty. She ran to the corral and leaned on the wooden posts, trying to get control over herself.

"I won't cry, I won't cry," she repeated, letting the words drone in her head like a chant until she felt that she had turned back the flood. She breathed deeply of the dry, still air, taking it in huge gulps, until hiccups seized her.

"Here, I thought you might need this." Jack came to stand next to her, holding out a cup.

Carrie couldn't look at him. She took the cup and drank

the water.

"Thanks."

"She's afraid for you, you know."

"She doesn't understand me or want to. If it weren't for her..."

Jack shook his head. "Do you really think if it weren't for your stepmother, Cody would write you the letter you want?"

Carrie nodded.

"Well, you're wrong. Maybe she can't help being discouraging because she's afraid you'll get what you want and you'll go away and get hurt or never come back, but it's not her fault if Cody won't help you. It's his choice, not hers."

"He would've helped me if she'd kept her mouth shut. He came to see me didn't he?"

"No, he didn't. He didn't know you lived on this ranch. He was just passing by, and he thought he could water his horse and get a meal here. He only remembered meeting you after you'd reminded him. Do you think he's spent the last six months mooning over you the way you have over him? Ha!" Jack slapped his thigh.

"You just shut up, Jack Rising," Carrie growled. "Shut up, go away, leave me alone. I don't care what you say. He did remember me. He just didn't recognize me at first."

Jack laughed, "You are so funny, Carrie, and so wrong. He sees you as this silly little girl dressed in boys' clothes, an oddity, something to tell the boys about when they're sitting around between rides swapping stories. That's all you are to him, a funny story."

Carrie was glad that the dusk had turned to night and Jack couldn't see her face in the shadows because she was afraid she was going to cry again. She was afraid Jack was right about Cody and right about her. She'd envisioned herself as a woman in love but she was really only a child, a stupid girl pretending that she was grown-up and ready for the world. But the world didn't want her. She felt her dream falling away. She turned her back on Jack.

"Go away, please," she said.

He didn't move for a moment, then he put a hand on her shoulder. "I'm sorry if I hurt your feelings, Carrie. I just hate to see you making a fool of yourself over someone like Cody, who can't see beyond himself."

Carrie shook his hand off. "Please go away and leave me alone now." She couldn't hold the tears back much longer.

Jack left quietly. When she heard his shuffling steps taking him up the porch steps and into the house, she bent her head on her arms and cried.

"Dead set on being a Pony rider, are you?" A soft voice spoke from the dark behind her.

Carrie stiffened. She wiped at her eyes and sniffed as discreetly as possible.

Cody sighed. "Well, all right, I'll do it. I'll write a letter. I hate to see a lady crying. But I'm warning you, too." His voice was kind but emphatic. "The Overland Pony Express has got the best men and boys to choose from for their riders. They're gonna laugh you right outta town. They'll be laughing at me, too, for giving my word, but that's all right, I guess. They ain't no way going to take you serious. If you think you're going to be a Pony rider, you're dreaming. You got that, girl?"

"I can try." The dream took shape again.

"Sure, sure, you can do that. You get me some paper and I'll write a letter saying whatever you think it oughta, and I'll sign my name to it. Just don't bet your whole pot on it, 'cause you'll lose, plain and simple."

"I have to bet on it and I have to win. I have to be independent or I may wind up being dragged back East."

"I do admire your gumption, girl."

Eight

Carrie stood at her bedroom window and looked out at the moonlit night. She pulled Cody's note from her shirt pocket, studied it intently for a moment, as if seeing it for the first time, refolded it carefully and returned it to her pocket. She turned back, glancing at her bed, which she'd arranged to look as if she were still in it. She gave the blanket a final tuck, picked up her boots and tiptoed out of the room and out of the house.

It had been two weeks since Cody had written the note. Four days ago the Pony Express had resumed service and she had waited impatiently for the first full moon to do what she knew she had to do. Now was the perfect time.

It took her only a few minutes to saddle Jack's mare and lead her from the stable. She longed to take Outlaw instead of the mare, but knew she couldn't. He had a job to do and if all went well, she might soon be a part of that job. She had one heart-stopping moment when she was sure she heard one of the men approaching. But no one appeared. Now, mounting the mare and leaving the stable yard, she knew she'd made it.

It was about eighty miles to her destination, Fort

Laramie, and Carrie planned to keep the mare at her fastest pace, stopping only when she had to, hoping to make it by the end of the next day.

"This is good practice," she said out loud. "This ought to show 'em I really can be a Pony rider."

The moon illuminated the road, making the going easy. She glanced nervously into the woods that lined the road. They were dense, pitch black and impossible to see into. Occasionally she heard rustlings, the source of which she could only guess at, making her shiver and urge Flag on faster. Look out for me, Pa, she prayed.

She rode through the night and well into the next day before the noon heat forced her to stop. The weather had shifted. There was a cool breeze and a definite feel of fall in the air, but at noon, with the sun straight over head, it was still summerlike and hot. Carrie was exhausted and knew Flag was, too. She led the mare into a grove of trees and, sheltered from the sun and passersby, Carrie fell sound asleep.

She awoke a few hours later with a stiff neck and a thirst which she quenched in a nearby creek. She let the mare graze at the side of the creek while she relieved her hunger with the few pieces of dried meat she'd brought, wishing she'd thought to bring more. Of course, when she'd left, food had been the last thing on her mind. There'll be food in Fort Laramie, she thought, as she saddled and mounted the mare. The sooner I get there, the sooner I'll get some.

The riding seemed endless and though she kept repeating to herself that it was good practice, when the buildings of the fort came into view at the end of the day, Carrie sighed with relief.

Fort Laramie was not enclosed within a stockade; its buildings were spread out in the open. The Indians were well aware of the power of the army and walls had never been necessary. The fort was rough, both in the structure of its buildings and in its populace. Soldiers on horseback and on foot moved about, busily engaged, while prospectors and trappers loitered. Indians, startling in their nearness, went about selling pelts or buying necessities with the money the furs had brought.

Carrie wandered, looking for the Pony Express office. She saw only a few women and no children at all. No one took notice of her, but then, why would they? With her long braids tucked under her hat, she must have looked like just another boy.

She finally found what she was looking for: a nondescript building bearing the sign, "Overland Pony Express

Office". She hitched the mare to the railing, took a deep breath, and with the note clutched in her hand, she went inside.

Joe Slade was no more charmed or impressed with her than he'd ever been. After a brief interview, he unceremoniously escorted her, once more, to the street.

Slade stepped back onto the office steps and looked down at her.

"I told you before," he said, tossing the crumpled note at her, "I will not hire a girl rider and that scrap of paper does nothing to change my mind."

"If I was a boy..."

Slade snorted. "You'd still be too young and inexperienced to be a rider for the Pony Express and too annoying for me to hire even if you weren't."

"But..." Carrie was ready to start her plea once more.

"I'm not going to stand here and argue with you any longer. Get it through your head, I said no and I mean it. Now, as luck would have it, you'll have an escort home."

"I don't need an escort," Carrie said sullenly.

"I think you do. I don't know how you made it here safely through eighty miles of Indian territory."

"I didn't see any Indians. You and your men have chased them all away, or starved them off, except these that you've got scared to death, who bring you furs. I can take care of myself." Carrie pulled herself erect.

"I think it's more likely that God looks after fools and little girls and you're both." He indicated a man lounging against a building across the road. "That's Pike, one of my men. He's going to Willow Springs and he'll see you home on the way. You won't have anything to fear with Pike around."

Except Pike himself, Carrie wanted to say.

He was a large, ugly man with a beaten, pocked face and small, mean eyes. He had thin lips that were drawn tightly together, forming a dark slash across his scowling face. Carrie was sure that face hadn't had a smile on it in a long time.

Thank God I didn't imagine him lurking in the darkness last night, Carrie thought, or I might have been too terrified to continue. Was this the sort of man that Slade had working for the Pony? She couldn't wait to get away from both of them.

The fort commander, Colonel Upson, and his wife, Emily, offered Carrie a hot meal and a room for the night and she gladly accepted. They were mightily impressed that she'd ridden so far alone.

"Is there some kind of emergency with your family?"

Mrs. Upson asked kindly.

"No," Carrie said, swallowing a mouthful of mashed potatoes and gravy. She smiled at them. "Everything tastes so good. I'm so hungry." She took her second roll from the bread basket and spread it generously with butter.

"Well, what in the world would make you come all the way out here?" Mrs. Upson persisted, eyeing Carrie's dirty shirt and trousers. "It was clever of you to dress like a boy for the ride. Safer, I suppose."

"I dress like this all the time. I hate wearing skirts; can't ride properly in skirts. I came to Fort Laramie to see if Captain Slade would hire me as a rider for the Pony Express."

Silence fell like a dead weight in the room. Carrie looked at their shocked faces and thought, uh oh, I shouldn't have told them. I never know when to keep my mouth shut.

They drew back from her after that and looked at her as if they had taken some strange creature into their home. Carrie found the house and their obvious disapproval stifling. She couldn't sleep in the overstuffed bed they'd given her and went out to the stable to sleep in the hay near Jack's mare.

The fort was quiet now and the streets were empty except for a few soldiers who were on guard duty. No one stopped her as she made her way to the stables. The stables were pitch black and she had to grope along the stalls until a soft whinny told her she had found Flag.

"Hello, girl," Carrie whispered. "Have they been taking good care of you? I thought I'd come out here so you wouldn't get lonely." She rubbed the mare's neck and kissed her soft nose. The next stall was empty and she took a couple of blankets from the stall walls, spread them out and lay down, more comfortable than she'd been in the Upsons' big fancy house.

She couldn't fall asleep, although she was as tired as she'd ever been. She lay there knowing that everyone at the ranch must be out of their minds with worry. It gave her a certain satisfaction that she was causing Anna worry, but she hated to trouble the rest of them. She should have left a note. Of course, Jack would figure out where she'd gone; she'd talked about it often enough. She knew they wouldn't be able to send anyone after her. Everyone was needed at the ranch.

She was finally starting to doze off when she was brought back to full wakefulness by sounds outside the stable. She froze. Her first thought was that her absence from the house had been noticed, and they'd come to bring her back like a prisoner.

But the door wasn't opened and she relaxed. It was probably one of the guards patrolling the fort. She would have dozed off again, but she could hear voices outside and the sheer stealthiness of the whispers made her alert with curiosity.

Two men were talking in low voices. The stable walls were thick and she had to strain to listen.

"You know what to do. Just like you did in Nevada." It was Slade, she'd recognize his oily voice anywhere.

"Yeah, we've been all through this. Remember, I want gold. Their paper money's no good to me."

Slade chuckled. "It won't be good to anyone before long. But don't worry, they'll pay and pay plenty."

"And if it gets messy?"

"Do what you have to do."

Their voices faded as they moved away from the stable. Now Carrie could only make out disjointed words— "California" and "that damn Lincoln" and then they were completely out of her earshot.

She wondered if the other man had been the scary looking Pike. What would Slade do if he knew she had twice happened upon his secret meetings? She shuddered just thinking about it.

She only wondered about them for a few moments;

within minutes she had fallen into an exhausted sleep.

She woke early and saddled the mare before going back to the Colonel's house. They never guessed she hadn't spent the night in their luxurious guest room, apparently assuming she had risen early to check on her horse. Carrie was sure that they found her odd and would be relieved to see her on her way.

From the moment they rode away from Fort Laramie, Pike acted as if he were traveling alone and Carrie was glad. They made good time with his steady pace, and Carrie got the feeling that he'd done a lot of traveling alone. Probably running from the law, she thought. During the day and a half it took them to reach Box Elder, she puzzled over what she'd overheard at the fort. She wondered if it was connected to the meeting Slade had had with the two dudes in April, the day the Express began. She didn't think it was Pony Express business, which Slade could have done in the open. She could hardly wait to get home and talk to Jack. Jack was pretty smart about things.

As it was, she didn't have to wait until she was home. They met up with Jack halfway between Box Elder and the ranch.

"We were going to send a posse after you," Jack said, the familiar teasing light in his sky blue eyes.

Pike didn't smile, didn't speak, barely took notice of Jack at all. He rode on, as silently dangerous as he had been for sixty-odd miles.

"Strange one, ain't he?" Carrie asked Jack, when she was sure Pike was out of hearing range.

"He sure don't say much," Jack replied. They headed back towards the ranch, following Pike at a slow distance.

"He was saying plenty last night, with Captain Slade. At least I think it was him. They were whispering together outside the stable and it was pretty late at night. They were up to something or my name isn't Carrie Sutton."

Jack considered her statement. "Just who is this Pike fella anyway? Does he work for the Express?"

"He's on his way to one of the stations down the line. Slade said Pike was one of his "men". I never hear him call Cal or you his "men". What do you think he meant by that?"

"I think it means that you'd better be darn careful when you're spying on Slade, especially late at night," Jack replied.

"I didn't do it on purpose."

"Nonetheless, if he were to catch you, there's no telling what he might do. Or have Pike do," Jack said.

Carrie grimaced. "I already thought of that. He sure is

scary looking, that Pike. He gives me a bad feeling. He makes me think of that saying, 'He's got a face only a mother could love'."

"And then only if the mother's a buffalo," Jack added. Carrie laughed.

"Well, whatever he does for Slade, I hope he's on the side of the Express and not against it," Jack said.

"Who could ever be against the Express?" Carrie was genuinely shocked by the suggestion.

"There are people who would use it for their own gain, and it wouldn't surprise me if Ole Slade were one of them. Which reminds me, what was Slade's reaction to the recommendation from the mighty Cody?"

"I don't know why you have to be so nasty ever time you mention Bill Cody's name," Carrie said.

"Maybe because he's such a blowhard and you're so gullible you can't see it. I guess I hate to see so much worship lavished on someone who doesn't deserve it."

"But he does deserve it! Unfortunately, like you, Slade doesn't think so highly of Billy either. He laughed in my face and threw me out of his office. I don't know what I'm going to do next. I'm losing time every time they put up another one of those telegraph poles," Carrie said.

"It won't be long before winter sets in and they'll have

to stop 'til the weather clears in spring," Jack reassured her.

"That doesn't give me a lot of hope."

"Why don't you just give up?" Jack asked.

"I don't give up, Jack Rising, and you oughta know that by now. It'll take more'n Captain Slade and some stupid telegraph to stop me." Carrie glared at Jack.

Jack laughed. "That's just what I thought you'd say and just what you needed to remember."

Carrie smiled and they rode in silence for a while. Yes, Jack was a smart one, she thought. The ranch came into view and Carrie thought she'd never seen a more welcome sight. It was a beautiful fall day, the kind of day that just makes you feel good to be alive. She reined in to savor the moment and the feeling. Jack stopped beside her. No words were necessary between them; Carrie knew Jack was feeling the same thing. She knew he had come to love the ranch and the valley almost as much as she did.

"Why didn't you tell me you were going?" Jack asked. Carrie turned and looked at him, raising her eyebrows.

"All right," he said. "I would have been against it. I know you think you're as tough as a man. I know for myself that you shoot and ride exceptionally well, but there are dangers you're not even aware of. And I don't mean Indians.

Anything could have happened to you riding all that way alone."

"I can handle myself."

"Yeah, yeah, so you say. I believe it, up to a point. Just do me a favor and don't go running off again."

"Oh, did you miss me?" Carrie asked mockingly. She was teasing but there was a look in Jack's eyes that told her she'd hit some chord in him. Suddenly she felt confused and a little unsure of herself. Then Jack smiled widely and a mischievous gleam came into his eyes.

"You stole my horse," he said.

"Ha! If I was going to steal a horse, I'd have stolen a *real* one, like Outlaw."

They bantered back and forth happily and rode in to a homecoming full of relieved faces and just in time for supper.

Nine

Carrie was happy when the Pony Express began to run regularly once again. There was a sense of urgency now as the presidential elections approached. The riders seemed to take special pride in making better time.

On the Sutton Ranch life went on in preparation for winter. Fall was the time for harvesting and putting up what little Anna's garden yielded, storing fire wood and drying meat. It looked to be an early and harsh winter.

Carrie wasn't interested in elections or war or getting ready for winter. There seemed no way she was going to become a Pony rider. While she racked her brain, she began to feel resigned, and she moped as she helped with the endless daily tasks.

Cal had wisely chosen Outlaw to make the election run and allowed Carrie to groom and saddle him on that November day.

Carrie knew that Outlaw's fondness for her had become apparent to everyone and that it was a source of much wonder that this fierce, barely tamed beast was so devoted to her.

Carrie loved talking to and fussing over Outlaw. He

searched out the bits of carrots, stolen from Anna's larder, that she kept in her shirt pocket.

"Is this what you're looking for?" Carrie pulled the carrot from her pocket. "You're a beautiful boy," she cooed, "and you're smart, too, aren't you? You do a real good job today and make me proud of you, all right? You'll be carrying important information. I wish I were riding you. We'd sure make a great team, wouldn't we?" She sighed. "I ought to just quit dreaming about it, like everyone says."

Jack walked up and leaned on the corral railing. "Got that horse 'bout ready?"

"Yeah, he's ready. Doesn't he look downright handsome?" Carrie asked with pride.

Jack stepped into the corral and ran a critical, knowing eye over the stallion.

"It ain't his pretty looks that got him this job," he said.

"Then it's lucky he's also the fastest, most sure-footed of all the Express ponies." Carrie put her hand up to Outlaw's velvety nose and he nuzzled against it.

"You know, you shouldn't get so fired up over one horse," Jack cautioned. "He isn't even yours."

"I've heard that before."

"It's the truth."

"Maybe I'll buy him."

"Maybe." Jack said. But he sounded skeptical.

"Hey!" Cal called across the yard. "Sorry to break up your party, but there's a rider due soon and I believe he'll be expecting a fresh horse to carry on the glorious news of Lincoln's presidential victory."

"We're coming right now, Cal." Jack called back. He turned back to Carrie. "Cal's positive that Lincoln's won the election. He's giddy at the idea of a war with the South."

Carrie smiled to hear the word giddy applied to Cal.

"Jack, I mean now!" Cal shouted.

"Don't worry," Jack called. "We'll be there before the rider."

As it was they had to wait; the rider was late. Minutes and more minutes passed. There was no forewarning of hoofbeats on the road. Outlaw began to fidget and Carrie tried to soothe him but she was nervous, too. What could have happened to delay the rider? She didn't like this. The mail shouldn't be late today, not with such important news. Jack passed a pistol, required since the Indian uprising, from hand to hand. Cal paced, muttering under his breath.

Anna joined them on the road. "I've been waiting at the house for someone to come tell me the election news. I thought you must have forgotten about me. Shouldn't the rider be here by now?"

"He's late," Jack said.

"It ain't like Petey to be off by even a minute," Cal said.

"Something's wrong," Carrie said. "Look, even Outlaw can sense it. Maybe he's not coming."

Jack raised his hand. "No, listen, he's coming now."

They heard the hoofbeats. Suddenly the rider appeared, racing at breakneck speed, galloping toward them.

Anna screamed. Carrie shouted, "He's not going to stop!" Jack leaped to her side and together they pulled the excited Outlaw off the road.

The horse and rider were barreling down on the petrified Anna, who stood, transfixed, watching the horse getting closer. Without thinking, Carrie dashed onto the road and grabbed Anna, pulling her out of the way just as the horse was upon her.

Cal threw up his hands, waving and shouting. The horse, spooked, veered suddenly, dumping his rider on the road. The horse trotted off a short distance and stopped, its sides heaving, its mouth dripping foam. The rider lay motionless. Cal and Jack ran to the fallen man. Anna turned to Carrie.

"Carrie, I..." she began.

"I would've done it for anyone," Carrie said.

"I don't know what happened. I couldn't move," Anna

said. Her whole body still trembled.

"Yeah," Carrie said. "I've seen rabbits act the same way in lightening storms. Too scared to move."

"Well, I'm glad that you're a quick thinker. Thank..."

Carrie interrupted her. "Forget it." She left Anna and went to the men, clustered around the rider. He lay face down, a dark stain spreading across the back of his jacket.

"Is it Petey?" Carrie asked.

"I don't know," said Cal. "Here, Jack, help me turn him over."

Jack handed the gun to Carrie and knelt next to the man and he and Cal gently turned him over. Cal and Jack inhaled sharply. Carrie just stared, taken back to the day her father was brought home, with the same sort of dark stains and torn clothes where bullets had ripped them apart. But this man, Petey, a rider they'd seen weekly since April, wasn't quite dead. Not yet.

Petey's eyes flicked open. He stared, but he obviously did not see. "Two of 'em. Road agents. I told 'em, weren't no money in the bags, just the news about Abe. But they..." He coughed and red spittle fell from his lips.

"Don't try to talk, Pete." Cal said.

Petey gripped Cal's arm. "Where's my horse? I gotta..."

"The mail will get through," Cal said, "Take it easy."

Petey fell back, barely breathing. "They...they'll be waiting...warn..."

"We have to get this man to the house and send to town for the doctor," Anna said.

Her words seemed to jar Cal and he took control. "Hank, come here and help. We'll carry him to the house. Carrie, take the horses to the yard and put the mailbag on Outlaw. We'll get Petey in the house and then I'll finish the run."

"Time's wasting, Cal," Carrie said.

"Don't I know it? So, get going."

Carrie took Outlaw's reins from Hank and retrieved the other horse from where it had wandered a few yards away. She felt a fevered, high-pitched excitement. Cal wasn't the one to take the mail on to Deer Creek; he was large and heavy. Even Outlaw would be slowed down under such a load. Jack, with his game leg, was out of the question. That only left the best rider on the ranch, herself. She ran the rest of the way to the corral.

As she was tossing the mochila across the stallion's back, she had an idea. If there were road agents waiting to make another attempt at stealing the mail, she'd be ready. She ran into the stable and grabbed her practice mochila, an old saddle blanket, and her hat. In minutes she was ready. She tucked her braids under her hat, pulled the gun from her waistband and checked its loads.

"I'm going to trick those murdering varmints," she said to Outlaw, who looked at her with his large, understanding eyes. "I don't guess they're the ones who killed Pa, but they're just as bad as the ones who did, and they're not going to get this mail if I can help it. You know what, Outlaw? I can help and prove a thing or two while I'm at it." She pulled herself into the saddle.

Anna was leading the men towards the house. She stopped at the sight of Carrie on Outlaw.

"Carrie, where do you think you're going? Stop right now," she said.

"I've never listened to you yet, and I don't guess I'll be starting now. And I'm not going to Pennsylvania!" Carrie shouted, as she urged Outlaw to pick up his pace.

"Get off that horse," Cal demanded. "I'm the station attendant here. I'm the one to go."

"Carrie, this is no practice game," said Jack.

"I know what it is, it's my chance and I'm taking it." Carrie clicked her tongue and Outlaw responded, cantering past them easily as they stood gaping at her.

"Carrie, for God's sake, there are thieves and murderers on the road. Please!" Anna pleaded. "Hank, do something! Jack, stop her!"

Carrie turned to look back at them. Jack was looking after her with admiration and fear and resignation. She saw him turn to Anna and shrug. "How?" he asked in answer to her pleas. Carrie smiled and rode on.

Ten

Carrie flew along the road, exhilarated but alert, her hand on the handle of the gun tucked in the waistband of her pants.

Suddenly two men, kerchieves wrapped around their faces, stepped onto the road and raised their rifles. Carrie pulled back on the reins and Outlaw came to a rearing halt in front of the men.

"Hold!" shouted the larger of the two. "Hands up, Pony rider. We want what you're carrying. Don't give us no trouble."

Carrie spoke, deepening her voice. "I carry the U.S. Mail and it's hanging for you two if you interfere with me."

"Oh, you're a brave one, I see. Well, we don't want you, boy, unless you force us to call in your checks. We only want what you carry."

"It won't do you any good to get the pouch. There's nothing valuable in it," Carrie said.

"We'll be the judge of that, so throw us the bags or catch a bullet. What's it to be?"

The two men stood menacingly in front of Carrie, brandishing their rifles. Carrie shrugged and began to slowly pull the saddlebags from the saddle beneath her. The men's stance relaxed.

"You'll hang for this," Carrie said.

The big man laughed. "We'll take our chances on that."

Carrie raised the bags in one hand. "If you want them, take them."

She hurled the mochila at the head of the big one, who dodged, snarling at her and turned to pick them up. Carrie pulled her gun loose and fired at the other, catching him in the shoulder. She drove her heels into Outlaw's sides and rode directly over the man who had stooped to pick up the bags. The horse knocked him over; for a fleeting moment Carrie was certain Outlaw was going to fall on top of him but he quickly recovered and bounded away. The fallen man scrambled to his feet and fired after her.

Carrie heard the shots behind her but ignored them, confident of her safety. Her hat fell back from her head and her braids caught in the wind and flew out behind her. She took one last look behind and saw the big man watching her, recognition and astonishment in his mean eyes. A shiver went through her. Pike! she thought.

Carrie bent low over Outlaw's neck, urging him on faster. She knew this road would take her right to the Deer Creek station and that Outlaw knew the trail. She wanted to make up for the lost time. Adrenalin pumping through her veins, the cold wind in her face, Outlaw's powerful strides beneath her, Carrie threw back her head and laughed and shouted with the joy of it.

She made Deer Creek Station in record time. Two men stood waiting impatiently, a big, muscular roan stallion held between them. They were yelling at Carrie before she'd pulled to a stop.

"Yer late! What's the news?"

"Hey, you ain't Petey."

"It's a girl!"

Carrie jumped from Outlaw amid their surprised faces. "Now's not the time for explaining; there's lost time to be made up," she said.

The older of the two, a large man with a bushy dark beard that was going gray, motioned to the other, a thin fellow who kept opening and closing his mouth as if shocked speechless. "Joe, grab that mochila and get on Flame and get a going."

"Wait, I can do it," Carrie protested. "Let me finish the run."

"Joe, do as I say. Girl, I'll talk to you in a minute."

Joe went to Outlaw's saddle and stopped, confused. "Hey, where's the mailbag?"

"Petey White got shot by road agents and I figgered they might have gone on ahead to catch the next rider, so I tricked them." Carrie loosened the blanket from where she'd tied it on the back of the saddle and unrolled it. The mochila fell to the ground. Joe grabbed it up and was on the roan in seconds. Starting to pull away he asked, "What's the election news?"

Carrie grinned. "Abe Lincoln," she said. Joe was off, tearing down the road and out of sight.

The bearded man looked at Carrie with admiration and bewilderment. He motioned to a red-haired young man who had come out from the cabin and was standing nearby, listening. "Woody, take the horse and see to him." He turned to Carrie. "And, girlie, you've got some explaining to do." He led her into the relay station cabin.

This was one of the stations that has been built quickly when the Express had begun. It was a crude one room cabin with bedrolls on the ground, a small area for cooking and a table. The man motioned for Carrie to sit down. He poured her a cup of strong coffee and told her his name was Jud and that he was the station attendant. Carrie began her story. She scarcely noticed the man called Woody come in and quietly sit down.

She told them how bad off Petey had been, how she'd

had the idea to use her fake mochila and how she had fooled the bandits. She didn't tell them she thought she had recognized one of the men. When she had finished, Jud stared at her for a long moment. "Took a lot of grit to do what you did, girl."

"You must have your folks worried plumb to death," Woody said.

"How's that stallion?" Jud asked him.

"He's a strong one, got more stamina than most. He's kind of tuckered, but he ain't done in."

"Could he make it back twelve miles if he goes easy?"

"Sure," Woody replied. "She oughtn't to ride back alone."

"I know, I'll go along with her," Jud said.

Carrie cleared her throat to get their attention. "I thought maybe you'd want me to take the return mail."

"Don't worry, we've got someone to do that," Jud said.

"But I could do it."

The station attendant looked at her and grinned. "That I don't doubt."

They met a fearful, desperate Jack on the way.

"Jack, hey there, Jack!" Carrie called, "What are you doing, Jack?"

"What do you think I'm doing? I thought we had an

agreement." His voice was stern, but she could almost hear his relief.

"There wasn't time to discuss it with you and you know it. Anyway, I'm all right, see? And I got the mail through. This here's Jud from the Deer Creek station."

There were introductions and thanks and Jud turned back toward Deer Creek.

"Good luck, Miss Carrie, maybe I'll see you again."

"Count on it," Carrie said.

She and Jack rode slowly back to the ranch. Carrie was still reeling from the excitement. But somehow inside of herself she felt a calmness, a rightness. She *was* going to be a Pony rider.

"You know something, Jack? It was like flying, like I knew it would be. Like riding on the wind, like in my dreams." She paused, pulling Outlaw to a stop, and faced Jack proudly.

"I proved something, didn't I?"

"I reckon you did," said Jack.

Eleven

The first snowfall came a few weeks later, at the end of November, dropping more than six inches in a matter of hours. The sky stayed gray and dismal for days, and the temperature dropped by degrees daily. There was every indication to Carrie that this was to be a very bad winter, and Hank's arthritis, slowing him down and making him groan with the pain of it, confirmed it.

Carrie remembered her father telling her how hard the winter months in the Wyoming territory were for everybody there; white man, red man and wildlife all felt the strain of months of freezing weather, the lack of food and the immobility. The men and Carrie made more frequent trips into town on the good days, for soon there wouldn't be any good days. There was more work, which Carrie hated, preparing for the days and weeks when there would be no work, no activity, but keeping warm indoors. The horses' coats began to get rough and shaggy, and Hank's arthritis continued to worsen.

But the Pony Express defied the elements and continued to run on schedule.

Returning from a trip to town, Hank and Jack brought

news that South Carolina had seceded from the Union and war was inevitable. This excited Cal to no end, and Carrie and Jack agreed that he was going to be impossible to live with.

One day in mid-December, like a pre-storm premonition, Joe Slade made an unexpected visit.

Carrie and Jack stayed behind in the stables after Slade had made his usual rudimentary inspection. Jack sat on a bale of hay outside of Outlaw's stall, while Carrie ran a brush over the stallion's already perfectly groomed coat.

"Did you see the way he glared at me?" Carrie asked. "He hates me, he really does."

Jack pulled a piece of hay from the bale and chewed on it. "He did seem to be acting more strangely than usual."

"But why? Just because I want to be a Pony rider? He acted like I'd done something to him."

"Maybe it has something to do with the ride you made to Deer Creek. He'd have heard about it by now."

Carrie shook her head. "Why would it make him mad? I saved the day, didn't I? I didn't hurt the Express, I helped it. He didn't even say a word about it. He might've thanked me or something."

"Maybe he's angry that you saved the delivery. We already know he's up to something, but what? And what purpose would it serve him if the mail didn't go through?"

"It wasn't just mail that day, remember, it was the results of the election," Carrie reminded him.

"I remember."

"Why wouldn't he want that news to go through?"

Jack shrugged. "No one said he didn't. Do you remember that meeting you spied on that Slade was having with those two men?"

"Sure. But I couldn't hear anything they said."

"Well, was it that you couldn't hear distinct words? Could you hear their voices at all? Could you tell if they had accents?" Jack was frowning as he asked the questions.

"What kind of accents?"

"Could you hear their voices or not?"

Carrie thought about it for a moment, trying to remember. "No, I couldn't hear a thing. They were too far away. But I swear, it looked like they were making some kind of deal. Slade drew something in the dirt at their feet, a map maybe or a plan, and afterwards they all shook hands like they'd come to some agreement. And those strangers seemed awful happy."

Jack looked lost in thought. Here she was trying to solve a puzzle and Jack wasn't even paying attention.

"Jack," she said, annoyed, "Are you listening to me?"

"Tell me again what you heard in Ft. Laramie."

"Something about California and about how whoever Slade was talking to should do the same thing he'd done in Nevada. And something about the Confederacy. And they cursed Abe Lincoln. I'll bet Slade was talking to that bad looking fella Pike. And I'm almost positive that Pike was one of those hold-up men."

"But you only saw his eyes." Jack reminded her.

"I'd never forget those eyes, Jack. They're killer eyes. Maybe we should tell Cal about this. Maybe somebody ought to tell the Pony Express owners."

Jack shook his head. "I'd like to have more information first. I'm just wondering what the Confederacy has to do with Slade."

Carrie shrugged. This was all very confusing and mysterious to her. All she knew for sure was that Slade stood in the way of her Pony riding ambition and she didn't like him any more than he did her. If he was up to something illegal she'd sure like to be the one to find him out and see that he was brought to justice.

"I smell hot biscuits, Carrie," Jack said. "I'm too hungry to try figuring this out. Let's go in."

"Do not let your guard down in regards to the Indians."

Slade was saying as they entered the warm kitchen. "I think my men and I have done a good job of clearing them from this area, but there are probably some still lurking around. My opinion is, if you spot any, shoot to kill and let's be rid of them."

"Doesn't that seem unfair, Captain Slade, since this was their land to begin with?" Anna said, with obvious dislike.

"The Indians are like the wildlife of this area; they must be thinned out to make the land livable for us," Slade said. "Settlers can't feel safe on the range, knowing Indians could attack any time, without provocation, stealing their stock and killing their families. They really are like wild beasts, and it's kill or be killed."

Carrie leaned forward toward Slade, eyes blazing. How she hated Slade! "That's not what Bill Cody said. He knows the Indian pretty good and he says they want to live in peace as much as we do."

Slade sneered at her. "Cody doesn't know anything except storytelling. What's he done for the Indians? He doesn't care about the Indians, he cares about Bill Cody. He's not as wonderful as he would have people think."

"Sure he is. He's the Boss Rider, isn't he?" Carrie would not tolerate slurs against Cody.

"He's no 'Boss Rider' to me," Slade replied. "He'll probably quit soon enough, like so many of the big talkers are doing."

"Pony riders, quitting?" Carrie's anger was replaced with amazement. She wanted so to be one–how could they quit?

"Well, Captain, you sound kind of satisfied that riders are quitting," Cal observed.

Slade turned his nose up as though something smelled bad. "I'm disgusted, of course. Just when they're needed the most, they're finding the job too tough or else they're taking off to join the army."

"And what's the latest news on that?" Cal asked eagerly.

"Nothing that you don't already know. There is a strong feeling that the southern states will soon be forming their own nation," Slade said.

"And what of the western territories and Mexico? Have you heard what stance they'll take?" Cal asked.

"California is a free state. I suppose that means it will go with the North," Anna said.

"That remains to be seen, little lady," Slade said. "There is a powerful Southern sentiment there."

"I think we should make the Western territories into an independent nation and just stay out of it," Jack said.

"I suppose that's to be expected from someone who can't fight," Slade said.

Jack jumped to his feet. "I can fight as well as the next man! I just don't give a hoot whether the Union is dissolved or not. But a lot of people are going to die over this thing."

Anna turned to Slade. "I don't know about the west, Mr Slade, but I'm from Pennsylvania and the thought of my sisters' husbands and sons going off to war sickens me. I'm a teacher and I've studied and taught about wars, and one thing is for certain; they are good for nothing. I oppose this war with every fiber of my being."

"It's always cripples and women who oppose wars," Slade said.

Carrie stood up, pushing her chair back with such force that all eyes turned to her. "And then there's some who welcome war for what they get out of it, like you! It's not just Indian lives that you don't care about; you don't care about anyone's life except your own!"

"Carrie!" Anna said.

Carrie whirled to face Anna. "Well, are you going to let him talk that way?"

Anna looked stunned. "No, of course not," she said gently, in a tone Carrie would use to sooth a nervous horse. "Why don't you and Jack get Mr. Slade's horse ready? He'll be leaving now."

"I beg your pardon, Madam, but this is a relay station for the Pony Express, of which I am an officer. I'll stay as long as I like," Slade said.

"No, Mr. Slade, *this* is *my* home. The relay station, officially, is in the stable, where you may stay as long as you like," Anna said haughtily. Carrie, surprised, almost laughed out loud.

Slade rose, beady eyes glassy and hard with a tight smile on his thin lips. "In that case, I will ready my own horse. I wouldn't want to have the saddle sliding out from underneath me at some vital moment," he said, with a knowing look at Carrie and Jack.

"Good day, then, Mr. Slade." Anna dismissed him like a naughty pupil.

Slade gave them a mocking bow and left, leaving the door open behind him. A blast of cold entered the kitchen and cleared the air. The five residents of the Sutton Ranch looked at each other and grinned in satisfaction. For the first time Carrie gave Anna an honest smile.

"You know," Carrie said, "Slade likes people to use his title 'Captain'. Nobody calls him 'Mister'."

Anna smiled more widely. "I know," she said.

Twelve

"You heard what he said with your own ears," Carrie said to Jack a few days later. "The Express needs riders now. I've got to find a way around ole Joe Slade to get onto the Express."

"What would you do if you could be a rider?" Jack asked her. "You know this wouldn't be your home station. You'd have to go miles away and live with a bunch of strangers. Men strangers."

"Well, gee, Jack I don't think there's anybody stranger than you and I've gotten used to you, haven't I?" Carrie smiled up at him sweetly.

Jack laughed. "I'm serious, Carrie."

"All right, then I'll be serious," Carrie said. "I'll do what I have to do to be a Pony Express rider. I can do the job and I want what they pay. I have to show Anna and Hank that I can stay out here in the west. I'm *not* going to go back east and that's that. Besides, you know they're going to hurry and finish stringing those telegraph poles as soon as spring sets in, and then it'll just be a matter of time before the Pony's not needed. Then I can come back and live on the ranch and make it successful like my Pa would've done if he'd lived. I've got to do it for Pa. So just help me find a way, please?"

"Well, maybe something will happen when you least expect it," Jack said.

"What's that supposed to mean? Do you have an idea?"

"You don't need an idea, Carrie; you need a miracle."

Jack refused to explain himself but went around looking mysterious. Carrie was positive he was up to something, that he did have an idea, possibly a miracle, but for some reason he wouldn't tell her.

Weeks passed and with the steady stream of Pony riders to prepare for and endless chores as winter set in, Carrie forgot about their conversation. Until the letter came.

Letters from Anna's family in Pennsylvania would occasionally find their way to the ranch via stagecoach or a neighbor coming back from town. There were times when Jack or Cal would get a letter from home, but Carrie and Hank never got letters.

So it was quite a surprise when one day at the beginning of the new year, 1861, a letter was dropped off for Carrie by the Pony rider.

Jack sat perched on the edge of his chair smiling like a fox who'd been in the henhouse. "Well, are you going to open it?"

Carrie stared at the envelope in shock. It was addressed to C. Sutton, Sutton Ranch Relay Station for the Overland Pony Express, near Box Elder, Slade Division, Wyoming Territory. "It's from Mr. William Russell of the Overland Pony Express." Carrie looked at Jack. "Maybe it was meant for Anna."

"They wouldn't be writing to me," Anna said, walking up behind Carrie to look at the letter over her shoulder.

"For the good Lord's sake, open the gosh durn thing," Hank said, scowling at them from his usual place in front of the fire, keeping his arthritic limbs warm.

Carrie turned the envelope over in her hands. She looked for the proper place to tear the valuable thing. Something metallic and cold was pressed into her hand- Anna's silver letter opener.

"It occurs to me that they may have gotten news of your heroic deed last November," Anna said.

Carrie slit the envelope and pulled out two sheets of thin parchment. Carrie stared at the first sheet dumbly.

"What's it say?" Jack was squirming with anticipation. "Read it out loud."

Carrie shook her head and held the page out to Jack with shaking hands. Jack took it and handed it to Anna.

"Would you read it, Miz Sutton? Good practice for a

schoolteacher," he said.

Anna took it from him. "Why do I get the feeling that you already know what this contains?"

Jack smiled and shrugged.

"'Dear Mr. Sutton'," Anna read and paused. "'Mister'?"

"Probably a mistake," Jack said. "Read on."

Anna looked at Jack, bemused. Understanding was dawning in her eyes. "'Dear Mr. Sutton'," she read, "'Our sincere congratulations and deepest appreciation for your brave and daring delivery of a most essential mail packet. This was reported to us by Mr. Jack Rising, whom you are undoubtedly acquainted with. He receives our commendation for bringing your skills as a rider to our attention.

" Mr. Rising has informed us of your devotion to the Express and your trouble entering its employ because of your young age. We believe this to be a serious oversight on our part and as of February first, 1861, you are officially in the employ of the Pony Express. Congratulations again. You will be expected to uphold the rules and regulations of the Pony Express and should conduct yourself accordingly. You must deliver yourself to the Cassidy Station at Willow Springs on or before the third of February and be prepared to ride February fifth'." Anna's voice got weaker as the letter went on. Carrie and the men leaned toward her as she read on in a whisper.

"The Station Master at Cassidy Station will acquaint you with your route. Again, we thank you for your quick wits and courage in an emergency. We need boys like you in the Pony Express. Sincerely William Russell.'"

Carrie took the letter out of Anna's hands and waved it. "I can't believe I'm finally going to be a Pony rider!" she cried.

"I can't believe it either," Hank said drily. He looked at Jack. "You didn't tell 'em Carrie was a girl, did you?"

Jack grinned as he looked from Hank to Carrie, but when he looked at Anna the grin faded. "I just didn't see how it could matter. Carrie proved herself and she deserves a chance to do what she wants."

"I sure do," Carrie agreed. "But, I'll tell you, I don't know what I ever did to deserve as good a friend as you."

Cal put his huge hand out and took Carrie's, dwarfing it. "Congratulations, Carrie. Enjoy it while you can, because as soon as they found out they've hired themselves a girl, you'll be right back to dreaming."

"They don't necessarily have to find out she's a girl, you know," Jack said.

Anna suddenly found her voice. "Are you completely out of your minds? You would send a young girl out among

Indians and cutthroats? My God, Carrie, you're only six-teen years old."

"What, all of a sudden I'm a child? Remember, you said that I'm almost a woman and I should start acting more like an adult." Carrie stood defiantly, legs spread, thumbs hooked into her belt loops and chin raised.

"This isn't what I meant and you know it! Don't twist my words around. I am not going to allow such liberties with your well-being. How can I let you go off more than fifty miles from home and live with dirty frontiersmen?" Anna was shaking.

"Well I won't be wearing skirts and pinning up my hair and blinking my eyes at them, you know. I'll dress like I always do and I guess I'll have to cut my hair so they won't even notice me for anything but another boy riding for the Pony."

"No, Carrie, it's out of the question. Your father left you in my care. He would never forgive me if I allowed you to come to harm."

"It's not up to you!" Carrie stamped her foot.

Hank spoke quietly from his place by the fire. "Miz Sutton, you know I love Carrie as though she were my own and I've been helping to look after her since she was a sprig. And I reckon I knew her Pa as good as anyone, including yourself. Now, I know that when Carrie makes up her mind about something she's like a hound with a bone and she won't let it go. I know Seth encouraged that in her and took pride in all the things she could do. Especially those things that she could do as good as any boy." Hank stopped and took a deep breath.

"Carrie's made up that stubborn mind of hers to be a Pony rider and I reckon I was one who thought it was just a pipe dream. But she set her heart on it and she's determined to see it through and I say let her go."

Anna gasped in disbelief. "Hank!"

Carrie ran to the old man and threw her arms around his neck. "I love you, Hank," she said, hugging him tightly.

"Look, Miss Anna," Jack said, "you know I wouldn't want Carrie to come to any harm. I'll ride out to Willow Springs with her to see what the men are like and what the place is like. If it's too rough, I'll write another letter and tell them the truth, and that'll be that."

Anna turned disappointed eyes on Jack. "You're the one who started this."

"No, he's not," Carrie said, "I am and it's up to me if I go and I'm going."

"The telegraph's going to be starting up again before too long and it'll be put up so quick the Express'll be over before you know it," Cal said reassuringly.

"Don't say that," Carrie said in horror.

Anna wrung her hands and looked from face to face. "I wish Seth were here."

"So do I," Carrie said. "But he's not. If he was, though, I know he wouldn't try to stand in my way. He'd be proud to let me go."

"I don't know about that," Anna said. "I just don't think it's the right thing to do. I think we should write to Mr. Russell right away and tell him a mistake has been made so he has time to find another rider for the Cassidy Station."

"No!" Carrie cried, whirling on Anna. "I'm going and you can't stop me! It figures that my dream would finally come true and you'd be the one to try and stop it. You've ruined my happiness from the moment you came into our lives. You've known me all of two and a half years and you want to run my life. It doesn't matter this time, though, because you are not going to stop me. Do you hear me? You can't stop me!" She went to her room and slammed the door behind her.

Breathing hard, Carrie pounded her fists into her mattress until she began to feel a little calmer. She went to stand in front of the small mirror that hung over her dresser,

122

picked up one heavy braid and contemplated it. She would have to cut her hair, which saddened her because her father had set a large store by his daughter's long, dark locks. She brushed the end of her braid over her face, feeling its silkiness. She was going to miss it. But nothing, absolutely nothing, was more important than being a Pony rider. She knew her father would understand. She'd take the severed braids and bury them next to him up on the knoll.

There was a light knock on the bedroom door. Anna pushed it open a crack, saying, "Carrie? May I talk to you? Please?"

Carrie stayed at the mirror, holding her braid. She pulled a pair of scissors from the top drawer. Anna could watch as she made her transformation; that ought to convince her that she was serious.

Anna came into the room and after a moment's hesitation, sat on the edge of the bed. "Look, Carrie, I know how you feel about me. I'm an interloper on your territory. I don't belong here. Maybe things would be different if your father had lived, but I can't fit in now and I know that. You see, that's why I have to return to my home, where I belong."

Carrie turned to look at her, the scissors poised in her hand. "I'm not going with you, so you might as well get used to the idea. I'm going to be a Pony rider and I'll make my own way in the world, like my father brought me up to do."

A dreamy look came into Anna's eyes and she smiled slightly. "He was such a good man, your father. I miss him so much, you know. Well, maybe you don't know, but I do— oh how I do miss him."

"You don't know this, either," she continued, "but I was a rebellious girl. I didn't marry and have children like my sisters did. No, I wanted to be a teacher. I wanted to make *my* own way in the world. I wanted to learn everything I could and that's all I cared about. Like you with your horses, I was devoted to my books. Men courted me and my family kept pushing me at this one or that one, but none of them turned my head, none of them became more important than my classroom. Until I met your father. I came out here for an adventure. I assure you I wasn't looking for love and I wasn't looking to ruin your life. But I loved Seth the moment I saw him. I thought we were going to have a long life together, and that I would have children, brothers and sisters for you, and that we would all be very happy for a long time. It just didn't work out that way."

Carrie was astounded by this revelation. "I never thought

about it like that," she said.

"And I guess I never considered how important staying here on the ranch is to you," Anna said. "I guess I forgot what it was like to be an independent-minded person. I'm just so afraid for you."

"You don't have to be," Carrie said. "You and me, we've never gotten along and maybe a lot of it's been my fault. But you know how much I've wanted this. I've practiced hard and I never gave up wanting it or trying to get it. It's too bad if it upsets you, but I'm going to Willow Springs and I'm going to be a Pony rider."

Anna looked at Carrie sadly. "I know, Carrie, I know. That's what I came in here to tell you. That, and one other thing."

Anna stood and went to Carrie, taking the scissors from her hand. "If you really are going to do this job, then be Carrie Sutton, Pony rider, and be proud of it. If you take the job and do it well, then *you* take the credit for it, not some imaginary boy named 'C. Sutton'. What I'm saying is, don't cut your hair."

Carrie looked at her in amazement. Anna smiled.

"Jack and the others have assured me that you are very capable of taking care of yourself," Anna said. "So what's the point in cutting off your beautiful hair and pretending to be someone and something you're not?"

"You're not going to try to stop me?" Carrie asked uncertainly. "You don't think I need to cut my hair?"

"Look at yourself," Anna said, turning Carrie back to the mirror. "What do you see?"

Carrie shrugged.

Anna placed her hands on Carrie's shoulders. "I'll tell you what I see. Your face has matured this last year; it's lost its roundness. You have a woman's face— high cheekbones, long, thick lashes and a perfect little nose. You could cut your hair and try to pass yourself off as a boy— after all you are tall and thin enough— but you'd be the prettiest boy they've ever seen. What's the point? Be yourself and you'll be all right. Oh, and carry a loaded gun and don't go wearing skirts and blinking your eyes at the frontiersmen."

Carrie smiled. "That I won't. I just want to ride for the Pony and be the best rider that I can be."

Impulsively Anna put her arms around Carrie and hugged her stepdaughter for the first time. "You will be the best, Carrie, I know it."

Carrie stayed in Anna's embrace and realized that some dark cloud had lifted. Anna wasn't so bad after all; there was more to her stepmother than she'd given her credit for. What's more, she, Carrie Sutton, was finally going to be a Pony rider!

1861
The Adventure

❧

Thirteen

The Cassidy Relay Station, Carrie learned, had originally been a ranch but the owner, Samuel Cassidy, had had a difficult time with it and, tiring of the isolated life, had sold it to the Butterfield Overland Express to be used as a stagecoach relay. It made a good relay station as it was large and comfortable and the house and stables were well built. The stone house had withstood Indian attacks and the harshest weather; it stayed cool in the summer and the pot belly stove and huge fireplace kept the building nicely warm all winter.

"What are you, an Injun boy?" was the first thing Carrie heard as she entered the house. Her braids were hanging proudly below her shoulders, something the station attendant had not seen on a Pony rider.

"No, I'm not an Indian," Carrie said. The station attendant's eyes widened. He was a tall, thin man and his eyes seemed to bulge from their sockets.

"Glory be," he said, shocked. "It's a girl."

Jack came in behind Carrie. "She's a Pony rider," he said.

"There ain't no girl Pony riders," The attendant said emphatically.

"There is now." Carrie handed him the letter. "Here's proof from Mr. Russell himself."

The other men crowded around, scrutinizing the letter.

"Seems to me this letter is to a boy named C. Sutton," The attendant said.

"I'm the only C. Sutton there is," Carrie said.

"Hey, wait a gosh darn minute." One of the men looked at Carrie excitedly. "Are you the gal that took the mail on to Deer Creek after Petey got shot? It was the delivery of the Presidential results, right?"

"That's her," Jack said proudly.

"I think this is a legitimate letter, Ben. You know, I told you about that girl. I heard it from Luke over at Liberty and he got it straight from Judd at Deer Creek."

Carrie nodded. "I know Judd. He'll vouch for me."

"I'll handle this, Curtis." The man called Ben, who was obviously the one in charge, eyed Carrie suspiciously. He moved his gaze to take in Jack. "And what are you, her chaperon?"

Jack laughed. "Carrie don't need no chaperon except

the ones she carries in her holsters. She's a dead shot."

"Is that right?"

Carrie realized that Ben, for all his boniness, had a stare that could intimidate a mountain lion and he was using it full force on her. She swallowed hard, trying to regain some of her confidence. Jack put his hand on her shoulder and his reassuring touch made her straighten up and square herself. She would not let Jack down.

Carrie knew that, if not for his lame leg, Jack would have been the one riding for the Pony. And he would have been good, too. He might even have been better than Cody, she thought traitorously. Inspired by Jack's belief in her, she decided to adopt a firm attitude with the men.

"Where's my bunk? I want to set my things down and then I want to look at the stock you have here and I need to get the route mapped out for me. Tomorrow I'll take one of the horses and ride it so's I can get to know it."

"Whoa there, little lady, you're getting ahead of yourself, ain't you?" Ben said.

One of the other men stepped forward. "Did Joe Slade approve of this?" he asked.

Carrie dropped her bag with a thud. She wanted every man in the room to pay careful attention to what was going on. She pulled herself up to her full height and stuck her chin out in a pose that all those on the Sutton Ranch would have recognized.

"Captain Slade was informed by letter, as that one plainly states. If he's got a problem with it, he won't get a chance to voice a protest 'til spring thaw. Right now the Express needs riders more than ever and I aim to be the best one they got."

"And I wouldn't try to stop her," Jack added.

"I say let her stay, Ben" the one called Curtis said. "This little girl will quit quick enough when she gets a taste of a rider's life."

Jack laughed. "You don't know Carrie Sutton."

Ben turned to the other men and shrugged. His voice held a mixture of resignation and wonder. "Well, boys, show her to her bunk and take her out to see the stock. We got work to do."

Then he stopped and turned back to Carrie. "But first I reckon there's a duty I have to perform. Dave, go get me that Express book."

A few minutes later, Ben intoned and Carrie repeated, " I, Carrie Sutton, do hereby swear before the Great and Living God, that while I am an employee of Russell, Majors and Waddell, I will, under no circumstances, use profane language; that I will drink no intoxicating liquors;

that I will not quarrel or fight with any other employee of the firm, and that in every respect I will conduct myself honestly, be faithful to my duties, and so direct all my acts as to win the confidence of my employers. So help me God."

"And God help us," Ben added.

Carrie adjusted easily to life at the station, feeling perfectly comfortable in the company of men, and she thought they sometimes forgot she wasn't one. She surprised them by being fearless, quick and tireless. She thought the men at the Cassidy Station and the ones along her route were gaining a healthy respect for her. She was proud of her work.

Her first few weeks as a rider were overshadowed by a terrible snowstorm. Hank's arthritic predictions came true; it was turning into one of the worst winters that Carrie could remember. The trail was buried under several feet of snow. New trails had to be broken on almost every run, making the ride slow and dangerous. Carrie didn't care about the danger, but she felt impatient at the slowness of the rides. She often thought, especially on the night rides, that if the worrisome Anna could see her, she'd faint dead away.

The snow blotted out the landmarks, and there was always the possibility of going over the trailside into a canyon. In some places Carrie had to dismount and lead the pony, which truely tested her forbearance. She learned to keep an eye on the tall weeds that showed up through the snow drifts on either side, marking the trail.

But the horses she rode were valiant and so was she, determined to prove herself. Icy wind roared around her and snow settled wherever it could get a hold. The wind swept up loose snow from the hillsides, and added to the stinging particles coming down from the low-hanging clouds. Still, Carrie managed to make good time.

All the practice that she had done under Jack's tutelage paid off handsomely. The men along the route cheered and applauded her flashy running mount. They didn't have much in the way of entertainment and Carrie knew that she was quickly becoming a favorite. She felt as if she were thought of as a particularly prized daughter and if, perchance, one of the men seemed to notice her beauty, the presence of her pistol was a quick reminder to put those thoughts out of his head. She was safe enough from the Express men, but not from the natural elements and the toll the long rides took—a toll that a lot of healthy young men had been unable to endure.

February came and more and more Carrie heard the

words "Civil War" and prophecies that 1861 would be the year that friends and families would be torn apart and people and property ruined. It seemed to Carrie as if no one spoke of anything except the coming war. The Pony riders kept all the little Express outposts updated. Sometimes, though, Carrie was sorry she had to hand the precious newspaper over to Ben, knowing that shortly he and Dave would be deep into an argument. Ben was from Missouri, Dave was from Georgia, and they were both itching to leave the west and get back before the war started. Meanwhile they fought it between themselves.

Carrie had only been riding for two weeks when the news came that the South had formed a new nation, the Confederate States of America, and had elected Jefferson Davis as their President. After that, all along the Express route, she heard strong opinions and saw tempers flaring.

February of 1861 brought hard times for all the creatures that lived from the land. Carrie often saw thin, desperate looking wolves eye her and her horse. She kept her gun drawn, wondering if they were hungry enough to strike. But they never did and, as dangerous as they might be, she felt pity for them.

During one snowy afternoon ride she thought she saw a dead wolf in a drift along the trail. She was on her way back to the Cassidy Station when she saw the dark lump in the snow. As she made her way past it, she saw several lean wolves slinking along the trees to the bundle that lay behind her.

"Must not be a wolf back there," she mused, "or else those others wouldn't be looking like they were on their way to supper." Must've been a deer or an antelope; wasn't big enough to be a buffalo. Pity welled up in her and she brought her horse to a stop. Fighting with her sense of duty to the Express was a picture of the wolves tearing apart a helpless and still living deer.

Carrie turned the horse back and drew her pistol. She could at least give the poor creature a quick death.

The wolves were almost upon the body lying in the snow. Crazed with hunger, made brave with starvation, they were beyond distracting with yells or her human smell.

The horse balked as Carrie tried to go through the wolves. There were four wolves, emaciated, but deadly ferocious. They were stalking the body steadily. Carrie came up behind a straggler, thinking to frighten it away with yells. It turned on her, jaws slavering. Her horse reared in fright. The wolf seemed blind with desperation and flung itself at the horse's flank. Carrie shouted and fired her gun. The wolf fell lifeless and, though there was pity in her heart, Carrie was glad she had ended its suffering.

The other wolves had stopped, pushing together and whining. It took another shot for them to reluctantly slink away.

She rode up next to the dark mound, intending to shoot it once and be off. She was acutely aware of wasting Express time. As she took aim she took a good look and realized it wasn't a deer or an antelope. What was it?

Carrie slid cautiously from the saddle, the pistol still in her hand, glancing nervously at the wolves who waited at the edge of the trees.

As Carrie approached the body she saw that it was not an animal, but a man. That explained the wolves' wariness in approaching it.

Carrie eyed the wolves to the side of her. They were whining loudly, almost howling, and Carrie knew there were many hungry wolves in the woods who would be attracted to those howls. She would have to act quickly.

There was nothing to do but hoist the man across the front of her saddle and get him to the station. Alive or dead she couldn't leave him to be torn up by wolves. How did a man come to be all alone out on the trail in the dead of winter anyway?

She blasted two shots into the trees at the wolves and

they yelped, retreating. Carrie led the horse to the man, talking soothingly. Snow had settled along his prone body. She bent and put her hands under his shoulder, pulling hard to turn him over onto his back. He was underdressed, looked as if he were near starvation and probably dying of exposure, but he was alive. And he was an Indian.

Fourteen

It would have been difficult for Carrie to get any unconscious man's dead weight across a saddle, but this Indian was thin, only skin and bone and not much weight, dead or otherwise. She managed to lift him and pull him across the saddle with a minimum of effort. He was an older man, maybe as old as Hank. Her heart went out to him, alone out in the cold and probably starving. Here, she thought, might be someone's grandfather. All the things that Cody had said back in October about the Indians and Slade and the winter came home to her with new understanding. She rode on the back of the saddle, her hand steadying the unconscious body in front of her.

Slade had strict rules against Indians; in essence his orders were, if you see one, shoot to kill. But Carrie had found that his orders were questioned by most in his division and blatantly disobeyed most of the time, but there were some who thought along the same lines as Slade. Carrie tried to remember if, among all the war talk, the men at Cassidy Station had ever voiced opinions on Indians. She couldn't remember if there had even been any conversation about Indians. If there had, she might know who she could trust to help.

She had to do something. They'd be waiting for the mail and she was getting behind now. She pushed the pony to make up for lost time and wished, for the hundredth time, that she was riding Outlaw. She tried to form a plan as she rode along.

Finally, she decided to detour around to the feed storage shed in back of the stables. There wasn't time to do more than slide the Indian from the horse, pull him into the shed and cover him with sacks. Then she jumped on the tired horse, backtracked and raced into the yard up to the waiting men.

She could feel their collective sigh of relief. In minutes the mochila was exchanged and the rider was on his way.

Ben walked with her to the house. "It's not like you to be late, Sutton. What's the story?"

"Had some trouble with wolves, spooked the horse a bit." Carrie smiled tiredly and, she hoped, convincingly.

"That's what kept you so long? We started thinking you'd slipped off the trail. Sure wouldn't think some mangy wolves could hold you up, not with your aim," Ben said.

"I don't just shoot every living creature I come across, you know. I can't shoot wolves just 'cause they're starving. I'd feel for anything that was starving. Wouldn't you?"

"I reckon I might unless it was me he was aiming to have for supper."

"Speaking of supper, I hope there's some ready 'cause I'm hungry," Carrie said.

While she ate she studied the men. Was Dave, the Georgian, the slave owner, an Indian hater? And Curtis, so loyal to the Express (and indirectly to Slade), would he shoot an Indian, even an old, starving one, on sight? She didn't know, hadn't known any of them long enough to take a chance. The Indian needed help. And she needed help to give him help.

"How's that stew?"

Pots, the cook, stood next to her, holding a steaming ladle over a black pot of rabbit stew. "You want a little more?" Pots never made a secret of the fact that he considered Carrie something of a pet.

Pots might help me, Carrie thought. She gave him what she hoped was an innocent smile and pushed her plate forward. "Thank you, Pots. It's really good tonight."

Pots grinned from ear to ear and dumped the contents of the ladle onto her plate.

"Hey, Sutton, where you going to put all that?" Ben called to her. "You know what they say, eat light, ride light." He laughed.

142

"Don't worry about my riding. Or my eating." Carrie stood and picked up her plate. "I think I'll go finish my supper with more civilized company. I'll be in the stables." She strode toward the door, her head held haughtily in the air. The men laughed and went back to their conversations and card playing.

The shed was dark and it took Carrie's eyes a few minutes to adjust. The Indian lay where she had left him. Carrie feared he might have died. He was breathing, though, and she relaxed a bit. He'd at least be safe until morning and by then she would hopefully have an ally. Right now he needed to be made warmer and fed a little.

She rolled the Indian in a horse blanket, wrapping it snugly around him. She piled several grain bags behind him until he was in a sitting position. He didn't seem to be unconscious as much as drowsy. His eyelids fluttered and his face twitched, but he never actually woke up. Carrie spooned stew broth between his lips and it slid easily down his throat.

It seemed to take forever to get a satisfactory amount of broth into the old man. By the time she was through, he had slipped into a calmer, deeper sleep. Carrie laid him across a pile of empty sacks, stacking full sacks around him, and covered him with more empty sacks. She left the potatoes and meat from the stew near enough for him to reach.

One thing was certain, he couldn't stay here. Besides the danger to the Indian himself, if Slade ever found out that this station had harbored an Indian, it would be bad for all of the Express men here. Carrie needed to find one man who could be trusted to help. She thought that man was either Ben or Pots. Ben always seemed fair and calm and Pots would probably do anything for her. But had either of them ever expressed a particular opinion about Indians? Darn, she just couldn't remember. Another thing was for certain— she had to get the Indian to the Sutton Ranch.

It was funny, but although Carrie and Anna had always been completely at odds, Carrie knew Anna would be there for her when she needed her. Anna and Hank would hide and care for the Indian until he was well. Jack and Cal probably wouldn't mind, either.

The card game was still going on when Carrie went in to the main house. In the corner fireplace, a pot bubbled on the stove and a coffee pot sat hot and ready. In the dead of winter and in the middle of a freezing night, Pots remained ready for the night wanderer, or, the night cattle guard, for Pots came from the life of chuckwagon cook for cattle round-ups. He dozed near the fire, softly snoring.

"Pots?" Carrie gently shook his shoulder.

"Carrie," Ben whispered, "Don't wake him up. I don't think he's slept in days."

"But—" Carrie began.

Ben shook his head, putting a finger to his lips. "Shhh, come over here. What's so important that you have to wake Pots up?"

"Nothing. It can wait till morning." Carrie exaggerated a yawn. "I better get some shuteye myself." She could see by the way Ben was eyeing her suspiciously that he wasn't mollified. She'd have to be more careful; Ben was nobody's fool.

She could hardly sleep that night, worrying about the old Indian. Curtis and Frank were always the first ones up, going out to the feed shed to get the food for the horses, and Carrie knew that she was going to have to get out there first and make sure the Indian was well hidden. She thought it was probably the longest night she had ever spent.

She was up and dressed before dawn, and breathed a little easier at the sound of the men snoring in the other room. Holding her boots, she crept to the fireplace. Pots must have gotten up at some point during the night and gone to sleep in his bunk. It was probably just as well. Before she told Pots or anyone, she'd better sound them out and take no chances with the old man's life. She filled a bowl from the stew pot that still hung over the fire and paused at the door long enough to slip into her boots. She was anxious, wondering what she'd find, whether the Indian had survived the night or if he'd still be where she'd left him.

He was there, sitting up, wrapped in the horse blanket. The stew meat and potatoes were gone. He observed Carrie through solemn dark eyes.

He wasn't quite as old as she had first thought, but he was an older man, somewhere between the ages of Cal and Hank, she guessed. His grey-streaked black hair lay loose and dirty down his back. His face was thin and serious and his eyes were calm and unreadable. His bones were all too near the surface, straining against the skin, stretched tight across the sharp planes of his face.

He's so thin, Carrie thought, dismayed. I wonder if he speaks our language. She held the bowl of stew out towards him. "I brought you some more to eat," she said.

He did not take the bowl; he gave no indication that he understood what she was saying or that he himself could even speak. Carrie set the bowl near him and wondered what to do next.

"I don't know how I'm going to make you understand this, but you'll have to hide out for awhile. And you can't stay here for long; the men are always in and out of this shed. So, see, you have to eat whatever I bring you as quick as you can so I can bring the dishes back with me, or the men might get suspicious." She waited, hoping for some kind of response. "I really want to help you, but I'm not sure what to do." The Indian stared at her without blinking.

Carrie crouched in front of him and tried making gestures as she spoke. "You were on the trail," she said, motioning to the outside, "and you were all alone." She hugged herself and shivered, trying to look cold and alone. "Are you from around these parts? Is your tribe around here somewhere?" She gave up trying to use sign language, unable to think of a way to act out what she was saying. She had to fight an urge to talk loudly and deliberately to him, as though volume and slowness of speech would make a difference.

A door slammed somewhere outside and that meant that Curtis and Frank were on their way to the shed to get the grain for the horses. Carrie stood up, fighting the panic that was starting to engulf her. Without thinking, she grabbed a feed sack and dragged it to the door.

She got the sack outside just as Curtis and Frank arrived. They both looked at her in astonishment.

"Hey, Sutton, what are you doing?" Frank asked.

"I couldn't sleep this morning and I thought I'd help out a little," she replied.

"What were you going to do, feed all the stock all by yourself? Shouldn't you be keeping up your strength for delivering the mail?" Curtis asked.

"I used to live on a ranch, you know, before I became a Pony rider. I'm used to feeding stock. Here, why don't you just take this sack and say thanks." Carrie tried to look indignant.

Curtis and Frank looked at each other and shrugged.

"If you're feeling a need to be helpful, that's all right by me," Curtis said.

"If you really wanted to be helpful, how about mucking out some stalls?" Frank added.

"Maybe I will, you never know," Carrie said, smiling at them. "Well, here's the grain, I reckon you want to get started feeding them ponies, right?"

"Yep, that's right, 'cept we always blend in oats in the morning, too," Curtis said. "I'll go get some."

"No!" Carrie jumped in front of the door. She smiled

again, wavering a bit as the men looked at her with amazement. "I mean, you go on and take the grain and get started. I'll bring the oats out."

"Don't be an idiot, Sutton. What are you trying to prove? Those sacks are too heavy for you." Curtis raised his hand as Carrie opened her mouth to protest. "We all know how tough you are, all right? But I'll get the oats."

There was nothing she could do but step aside and hold her breath. Well, now she'd know how Curtis and Frank felt about Indians. She followed Curtis into the shed.

In the gloom of the windowless building and with the sacks piled high around him, the Indian was out of sight. Curtis, unaware, grabbed a sack near the door and, glancing at Carrie, heaved it over his shoulder and started out.

"Well, are you coming?" he asked.

"Uh, oh sure, I'm right behind you." Carrie glanced back at the Indian's hiding place and trailed slowly behind Curtis.

It was another hour before she could get back to the shed to check on the Indian. To keep up the pretense, she helped feed all the horses. Passing through the house, she managed to slip some dried meat and a good sized hunk of bread under her jacket and, unobserved, she hurried back to the shed.

The Indian apparently hadn't moved the entire time, except to eat the stew. The bowl was empty. He watched through dark eyes that now seemed more alert. Carrie sat on the sacks near him.

"You don't have to worry, I'm not going to let anyone hurt you. I saved you and I'm taking responsibility for you."

He didn't look worried and there was not a bit of comprehension on his face. Yet Carrie felt comfortable talking to him. It was sort of like talking to Outlaw; she knew he never understood one word she said, and yet she always got the feeling that he liked listening to her. Of course, this was a person, and it was possible that he did understand her, but didn't want her to know it.

"My name is Carrie." She jabbed her finger into her chest. "Carrie, that's me." He did not change his expression. Carrie pulled the bread and meat from her jacket and held it out to him."You should eat. You have to build up your strength. Are you warm enough or do you need more blankets? It's good that you stayed down before. You need to stay hid just 'til I can get you to where I live. See, I used to live on this real nice ranch before I became a Pony rider. It's a small ranch, really. Jack says it's not much more than a farm. He just says that to get me mad, 'cause it ain't no farm, it's a ranch, and when Hank and I are through with it, it'll be bigger and better than ever. She could see the ranch in her mind; the sturdy brown buildings, the jagged rocks of the well, Anna's garden. She could imagine Outlaw in the paddock, waiting impatiently for her whistle, and she could see Jack, the usual crooked smile on his face, greeting Anna cheerfully as he came in to supper. Even Anna's face came to mind, her sharp blue eyes and rosy cheeks against her fair complexion, a wisp of blonde hair clinging to her damp neck. An intense wave of homesickness came over Carrie. She missed them all so much, even Anna. A tear surprised her by falling on her hand. She glanced up at the Indian and blushed, swiping her hand across her eyes quickly.

Had his expression actually changed? Was she imagining this, too, or was he looking at her with concern? She smiled reassuringly.

"Sorry, I didn't think I was going to get blubbery. I guess I miss being home more than I thought. But it's all right, because there's nothing I'd rather do than be a Pony rider. And if I wasn't one, then you might've been wolf food."

They sat there in silence for a few minutes, then the Indian stirred, letting the blanket drop from one arm as he reached out and took the bread. Carrie looked at him and their eyes met. She was sure she saw the barest glimmer of acknowledgement, a twitch on the side of his mouth that passed as a smile. He began to eat the bread.

"I think I'll tell Pots about you. Pots likes me— I can tell. He never married or had kids or anything and I think he's kind of adopted me. I think if I approached him just right, he'll help me figure out how to get you to my ranch. You look like you're getting stronger already. Maybe it won't be so long before you'd be ready to travel." Carrie grinned and said, unnecessarily, "What do you think?"

"I think you've gotten yourself into a load of trouble." A voice said from behind her. The shed door slammed shut with a bang and Carrie jumped.

"Ben!"

He stood glaring at her, his hands curled into fists against his hips. "Sutton, what kind of hare-brained thing have you done?"

Fifteen

"I couldn't just leave him to the wolves, could I?"

"This was the 'trouble with wolves' you had yesterday, I suppose." Ben was fuming, obviously trying hard to maintain control. "Very smart, Sutton. Should've known a girl rider was going to be trouble."

"Well, what would you have done, huh?" Carrie stood to face Ben, ready for a battle.

"It's not a matter of what I would have done, the problem here is what you have done. What could you have been thinking, bringing an Indian here!" Ben exploded. "You know the rules. I thought you were so fired up to be the best Pony rider that the Express has. How many riders do you think stop to pick up Indians? This Indian will probably ruin the lot of us!"

Carrie stared at Ben in amazement. "I didn't know you were such an Indian hater."

"I'm not, you fool, but Slade is and you know it. What if he finds out? Then this pet Indian of yours is going to be dead anyway and you'll be out of the Express before you can say 'war paint'."

"I'm not afraid of ole Joe Slade. I've never liked the

way he's dealt with the Indians. In fact, I don't care for Slade one little bit and I'd be glad to know that I helped out at least one Indian." And she wasn't going to let anyone hurt this one.

"And just what were you planning to do? How long did you think you could keep him hid in here?" Ben asked.

"I sort of figured if I could get him to my ranch, my folks there would look after him."

"Oh, that's real good thinking, Sutton. You must think a lot of your folks to put them in jeopardy." Ben shook his head at her apparent stupidity.

"Look at him, Ben, he's old and weak. He's all bone. He wouldn't hurt anyone."

Ben looked at her in disgust. "Yeah? Well, Slade ain't so old or weak. And he ain't fair-minded or full of mercy, either."

Carrie glanced back at the Indian, who was watching them passively. "Look, could we go outside and discuss this?"

Ben looked over at the Indian, too, and nodded. "Yeah, but my mind's made up. He's got to go. Now."

Carrie led Ben outside and stood for a moment shivering in the cold. Then Ben turned and walked toward the stables and, with a last backwards glance, Carrie followed.

The stable was warm and pungent with the smell of horses.

Ben sat down on a bale of hay and looked at Carrie. "I knew you were up to something when Curtis told me how you'd helped with the horses and acted so strange at the feed shed. And I saw you taking the jerky and bread." Ben gave a short, strident laugh. "And here I thought you'd gotten yourself a wolf pup."

"Please don't be mad, Ben. But what could I do? My Pa didn't raise me to turn my back on someone in need," Carrie pleaded.

"If you can't communicate with him, how did you plan on getting him to your ranch?" Ben asked.

"I hadn't gotten that far in my planning," Carrie said. "But, now that you know, maybe between us, we could come up with something. I was going to let Pots in on it. I thought he might help."

"Hmmph," Ben snorted. "It's a good thing you didn't. He used to cook for cattle drives, you know, and they got attacked by Indians more times than you could imagine. Pots definitely has no love for the Indians."

"Are you going to help me?"

"I guess I'll have to. But we have to tell the others; it's only fair. Besides, the only way I can figure to get that

Indian to your ranch is if one of us takes him in the wagon."

Carrie felt a rush of warm gratitude. "Oh, thank you, Ben. You won't be sorry. My Pa always said it was good fortune to help others."

"Well, I hope the other men feel the same way," Ben said.

"How do you think they'll take it?" Carrie felt apprehensive at the thought.

"I reckon we'd best go find out." Ben stood and stretched. He was obviously not anticipating a positive reaction.

As Ben had warned, it was Pots who objected most vehemently to the Indian, declaring that all Indians were horse thieves and murderers, and he looked at Carrie with disappointed eyes. Frank and Curtis were merely curious and wanted to see the savage for themselves. They all trooped after Carrie to the shed to have a look.

The Indian was gone. He'd taken the rest of the food and the horse blanket and vanished. A soft snow was falling, quickly obliterating any foot prints.

Carrie watched the men shrug and head back to the warm fire in the house. Ben placed an understanding hand on her shoulder before joining the others. She stayed at the shed, silently letting the snow fall on her, and said a prayer that the old Indian, whoever he was and wherever he was going, would be all right. She guessed she'd never see him again.

The riding became tougher as March wore on. The toughness was not due to the weather, which began to clear, but to the steady stream of California and Oregon-bound travelers on the trail. Carrie had been told that all trails were being used, but she resented their using the Overland Pony Express route.

Carrie was often compelled to leave the trail, breaking her way into the deep snow, in order to get past some pack train or wagon outfit. She would tear along, intent on bettering her schedule, and come around the side of a hill or out from a woods and run head on into a freight-wagon or pack wagon. Voices rose up in protest as she upset their westward flow and they cursed her for being a fool or a lunatic. And then they would invariably notice, as she made her way around them, her two, long, thick braids, and she would see their mouths fall open with surprise.

News of Carrie Sutton, the girl Pony rider, had begun to circulate among the western towns. Carrie was proud of that. If word had gotten back to Russell, Majors and Waddell, they showed no sign of it and never stopped her from riding. By their very silence, they showed their approval. "I'm doing what I set out to do," she would think. "I wish Pa could see me."

The beginning of spring brought Joe Slade. He came riding in a few days after the last snow storm of the season. He was making his first route inspection of the new year and he brought the latest news of the goings on in the country.

President Abraham Lincoln had taken office on the sixth of March and there seemed to be no doubt that there would be a war. "And it's a good thing for you that there are rumors of war," Slade told Carrie, ever arrogant and cold. "You'd never remain a rider otherwise, you and your sneaky backhanded tricks. Unfortunately a lot of our riders are heading home to the North or South to join the troops and prepare for war."

They were alone in the cabin and Slade was obviously seizing the opportunity to be hateful to Carrie. Well, she'd show him she was one person who could stand up to him.

"I would think you'd be glad that I turned out to be such an asset to the Express."

"I'll be glad the day your stepmother drags you back to Pennsylvania," Slade sneered.

"That ain't going to happen. I'm not leaving my ranch and Anna knows it."

"Isn't that a shame. Well, anything can happen here in the lawless west so you'd better stay on your guard."

"Are you threatening me? I suppose you could send your man Pike after me. Better disguise him as a road agent, though." Carrie stopped, afraid she'd said too much.

Slade's eyes had narrowed and he contemplated her silently.

"If you've got something to say, why don't you just say it," he said.

Ben came into the house then, followed by Pots. Carrie felt relieved. She had a feeling that it was not such a good idea to try to out-threaten Slade. He hadn't earned his ruthless reputation by accident. With Ben and Pots for witnesses, however, she felt safe enough to pursue their argument.

"I must confess, Captain," she said, "that I've wondered about Pike. I could've sworn he was one of the hold-up men the day Petey got shot."

A slow, evil smile spread across Slade's face. "He may have been. He turned renegade a while ago." Slade shrugged. "I try to hire trustworthy men, but I can't always be right."

Yeah, I'll bet you knew what you were doing when you hired Pike, Carrie thought.

"If Pike had anything to do with Petey's shooting, he'll be brought to justice," Slade continued. "I'm certain he's miles from here, though." He turned his back to her, dismissing her.

Slade spent the rest of his visit discussing the local Indian tribes. He made it a point to describe them as ferocious. Carrie listened, but she didn't believe a word he said. She, like everyone along the Overland trail, knew that the winter had been very hard on the Indians. They had barely survived being hunted by Slade and his men, the loss of their land and their food supply. Many did not survive, particularly the weak and the old. Those that were left were the young, strong and angry. They had caused some trouble, spirits high with the end of winter and a need to replenish their supply of horses. No matter what Slade said to the contrary, Carrie realized that they were not out looking for scalps, but rather for horses and food. It was Slade who was always making them look like cutthroats.

Carrie was glad when Slade was finally gone. She had wanted to ask about Cody. Was he one of the riders who had left to join the army? Was he still riding for the Pony? How was he? She never heard any word about him. But she wouldn't ask such things of Slade and subject herself to more of his scorn.

Carrie didn't think about Cody as often as she used to. Life as a Pony rider was full of adventure. Once in broad daylight, barreling around a turn, and coming upon an emigrant outfit, Carrie was fired upon. The bullet whizzed past, just missing her. She pulled her confused horse to a stop and whirled around.

"What did you do that for?" she demanded loudly, resisting an urge to swear.

A voice quavered from the wagon's interior, "We thought you was an Injun!"

Another time, on a night run in pitch darkness, Carrie nearly rode into a broken-down wagon which had been left on the trail. Apparently the owners were waiting until daylight to make their repairs. Luckily for Carrie, she had keen eyesight and managed to pull up and get around it in time.

It seemed to Carrie that she couldn't make a run without having to deal with travelers. Often, riding along a narrow trail, she would nearly run into a wagon train and would have to go off the road, along the side of a steep hill to get around. Although she was soothed by the people who cheered her in obvious admiration, she still cursed the precious extra seconds it took.

In spite of Slade's dire warnings, the Indians gave her

less trouble than the settlers in their dingy-topped, creaking wagons. Carrie often saw Indians as she rode, but was only chased a few times and then she easily outdistanced them on her well-fed, superior mount. They never fired at her and lost quickly interest.

Always, when she saw them, even when she was being pursued by them, Carrie thought of "her" Indian and wondered where he'd gone and if he had survived the winter.

Then, if the settlers and occasional Indian weren't bad enough, as the snow began to thaw, work began again on the telegraph and poles began to rise up like a row of corn across the plains and mountains, signaling the beginning of the end for the Pony Express.

Being a Pony rider was a tiring profession, Carrie was starting to admit to herself. As much as she loved it, she never seemed to get enough rest and it was beginning to tell on her.

One afternoon, making her return run to the Cassidy Station and eager for food and sleep, Carrie thought her tired eyes were playing tricks on her. Could that really be Jack there, waiting for her?

It was!

"Hey there, Carrie."

Her tiredness left her instantaneously. "I must be seeing

things, this can't be true. Is that really Jack Rising?"

He strode to her and caught her up in a quick, tight hug, then released her, smiling into her face. "It's good to see you," he said.

Carrie stared up at him, a grin crossing her face. "Good to see you, too, Jack."

"I brought Outlaw with me."

"What!"

Jack laughed. "First your eyes and now your ears. This Pony riding's starting to wear you out. Hey, where are you going?"

Carrie had spotted Outlaw, tethered outside the stable, and was heading towards him. She whistled and his ears pricked up. He hasn't forgotten me, she thought, jubilant. She ran the remaining distance and threw her arms around his neck, cooing and praising him.

His coat still had its winter shagginess and Carrie was soon covered in hair. She turned to Jack happily.

"I'm not complaining, but what are you doing here?" Then she knew before he could answer, just by the look on his face. "The telegraph?"

"Yep," Jack said. "The lines go all the way to Red Butte and the Sutton relay's no longer needed, so we're closed down. The stock is being divided up among the other relays or stage stations. I knew how much Outlaw meant to you, so I brought him here. I thought you might like something from home. I'll tell you, I had a hard time convincing Hank and Miss Anna that I was the one to bring this old horse to you; they each thought they should be the one."

The thought of crotchety old Hank or the feminine Anna riding the fifty miles to Willow Springs made Carrie laugh. "I missed you all so much, I wish they could have come," she said.

Strangely enough, she thought, she had even missed Anna.

"Really? Well, I guess absence does make a heart grow fonder," Jack said, his blue eyes twinkling.

"You sure haven't changed, Jack Rising, still a tease." Carrie sniffed. "You didn't mention Cal. How is he and what's he going to do, now that the relay's shut down?"

"Oh, Cal's gone on back East to join the army."

"Do you know if Bill Cody has gone off to war? Has he left yet?" Carrie's heart stopped.

"Now how would I ever have heard a thing about Bill Cody?" Jack asked stiffly.

Carrie thought he sounded hurt. Why would that be? Then she thought she knew; here she was asking after Cal and Cody and she didn't even know what Jack's plans were.

"What about you, Jack?" She asked. "What are you going to do?"

"I'm staying at the ranch," he replied.

Carrie was surprised by the relief she felt.

"I've written home to ask my two younger brothers to join me. You'll like them. They're not like me at all." He smiled.

"Oh, Jack."

"Miss Anna is still determined to go back east and she knows she won't be able to persuade you to go with her."

"I'm not going anywhere. I'm staying on the ranch —"

"I know, I know. We all know. You've always been very clear in your intentions. Anyway, Miss Anna agreed that she would feel better about leaving you here if there were more hands on the ranch. Of course, she'd prefer it if there could be a matron, or herself, there as well, to act as chaperon."

"What! I don't need a chaperon. I guess I've proven that, haven't I? What does she think I've been doing all these months, huh? I can take care of myself! Of all the—" Jack laughed and she stopped, sputtering. "What's so funny, Jack Rising?"

"You are still so easily riled. Can't you let someone care about you without getting your pride all in an uproar?"

"Well, I'll be all right without any old matron looking over my shoulder. And you can tell Anna I said so."

"It's none of my business, so you can tell her yourself. I've got something else I want to talk to you about that's more important." He stopped, watching Carrie as she stifled a yawn. "But you're looking tired out. Maybe you'd better go get some sleep. This'll keep."

"No, talk to me now, please. I don't have to ride again til day after tomorrow. I can sleep anytime. I don't know when I'll see you again."

Jack smiled. "You'll probably be seeing me real quick, as soon as the telegraph squeezes the Pony off the track and that won't be long."

"You don't have to sound so happy about it," Carrie said.

"Do you want to bicker for old times sake, or do you want to hear what I have to say?"

"I want to hear, tell me. Is it about Cody?"

"Don't you think about anything else? No, it's not about Cody. It's about Slade. That man that you rode back from Fort Laramie with, what was his name?" Jack asked.

"Pike?"

"Yeah. Do you still think he was one of the hold-up men?"

"I'm sure of it. Slade was here a while ago and I told

him I thought so, too."

"You didn't."

"Sure I did. And Slade said it could have been Pike, because he's gone renegade." Carrie was surprised by the look of concern on Jack's face. "What's the matter?"

Jack looked at her, his blue eyes dark. "Just seems to me if I'd been accused of a crime worth getting hung over, I might not want to stick around the area where I could easily get caught."

"For goodness sake, Jack, what are you talking about?"

"I've seen Pike."

"Where?"

"I've seen him twice, actually. I was riding home one day last week and I saw him heading up into the foothills about a mile out of town," Jack said. " And about a week before that, I thought I saw him going into the hotel in Box Elder. It was him alright."

"What? But Slade said..."

"He was lying." Jack paused.

Carrie watched him, understanding dawning in her. "You know something more, don't you? Tell me, what is it?"

"I don't know this for sure, but I think Slade's using Pike and some other men to give the Indians a bad name. There's been trouble along the Pony trail— some say desperados and Indians. But I think Pike and his men are be-hind it. I do not believe the Indians are doing the killing and burning. The army and Slade are out to get them; why would they bring more trouble down on themselves? No, someone's trying to make it look like Indians."

"Why would anyone want to do that? For what purpose? Just to make trouble for the Indians? It doesn't make sense." Carrie shook her head.

"It makes a strange sort of sense if Slade's involved. I think you should be on your guard. There's been talk of a secret society set up by the Confederacy to get control of California before the Union does. It could affect the out-come of the war. Slade could be in on it, and he could be trying to slow down delivery of information going west."

"How do you know all this? From Cal? Or did you fig-ure this out all by yourself?" Carrie asked.

"Oh, I know things," Jack replied mysteriously.

"How?"

"I'll tell you all about it soon, I promise. In the mean-time, be extra careful and keep a hand on your pistol when you're riding. All right?"

"All right. But you don't have to fear for me, Jack. I can take care of myself. You know what I did about those road agents last November."

"That's just it. That was the run that carried news of Lincoln's victory, and it still seems to me like an odd thing for robbers to want to steal."

Sixteen

Carrie was sorry to see Jack leave the next day. They had stayed up talking for hours and having him there made Carrie realize how much his friendship had come to mean to her. She told him about the Indian and he applauded her, making her feel that she'd done a good and noble thing. That's what was so great about Jack; she could tell him anything and he never judged or condemned her. She didn't want him to leave. Her only consolation was that Outlaw remained.

The day after Jack's departure she rode the stallion for the first time as a Pony rider. It was like heaven on earth for her. Outlaw was faster and more powerful than any other horse she'd ridden. He responded to her almost as if he could read her mind.

But, even on Outlaw, riding for the Express was becoming a strain, and she was beginning to feel exhausted. She never seemed to get enough sleep. And the homesickness she had felt when she saw Jack had not gone away. She found herself thinking of the ranch constantly.

Sometimes she would complete a run, not remembering certain landmarks and she'd realize that she must have fallen asleep in the saddle. But Outlaw learned the trail quickly and would not falter, keeping a steady pace. Carrie was convinced he was the smartest horse in the world.

Now as she rode, she passed alongside the place where the telegraph poles were being put up. The men stopped their work to wave and call out to her. She took her hat and waved it back at them.

They'll be to Willow Springs before long, she thought, feeling both happy and sad. I'll be going home soon, she thought, looking forward to it.

She was tired and the robust good health that she had always taken for granted was beginning to fail. She knew there was no loss of honor in it; many of the riders before her had been forced to quit due to ill health. Riding for the Pony, as Cody and many others had warned her, was a hard life. Still, she had proven to all of them and to herself that she was as sturdy, dependable and able as the male riders and she wasn't quite ready to give it up. Not yet. And yet, when she allowed herself to think about it, she had an ache gnawing at her. She wanted to go home.

Keeping in mind the things she and Jack had discussed, she stayed alert for disturbances along the trail. If someone, Slade or anyone else, was trying to disrupt the running of the Express for some devious purpose, she would stop them if she could.

Someone had tried to stop the news of Lincoln's election victory, but when the southern states had formed their new Confederate States of America, and elected their own president, nothing had happened to keep that news from reaching California. What could that mean?

Tempers were quick at the Cassidy Station as Ben and Dave fought a civil war between themselves and waited impatiently to be off to join their respective troops. They were evidence of an occurrence happening more and more as friend turned against friend in the name of their loyalties. To Carrie's tired mind they were acting like children squabbling over a toy.

Most of the time she didn't think at all except to wonder how she could squeeze in a few more hours of sleep. As tired as she was, it often took her hours to get to sleep. As she lay in bed, she would still feel the motion of a horse beneath her and be unable to relax enough to fall into slumber. And she never seemed to dream anymore.

One night, weeks since Jack's visit, Ben knocked quietly at her door. "Sutton, you awake?"

"Just barely, Ben. What is it?" She hadn't been able to sleep anyway.

"You've got company."

Carrie sprang out of bed and grabbed her jeans and shirt, throwing them on hastily. Jack! she thought eagerly.

"Hey there, Miss Carrie." It was not Jack, but Bill Cody who stood there, smiling.

"What are you doing here?" Carrie shook off her disappointment. Cody was *here*, visiting *her*! So why was she thinking of Jack?

He looked just the way she remembered him: blond and rugged and exceedingly handsome. The months of Pony riding showed on him, too. He was thinner and his face seemed lined. His eyes had shadows underneath them as if he didn't sleep enough, either. Essentially, he was just as she remembered. But did she feel the same as she used to?

Of course she did. She loved him. Didn't she?

"And I'm on my way to Fort Laramie," Cody was saying.

"What?" Carrie hadn't been listening. "I'm sorry, Billy, what were you saying?"

"I said I'm on my way to join the army and I thought I'd come on by here and say good bye to you and offer you my belated congratulations," Cody said.

"Congratulations?"

"On being a Pony rider." He peered at her. "Are you all right?"

"She's just worn out," Ben said. "She rides harder than anyone I know."

Cody nodded. "I thought she'd be that way if she ever made it onto the Express." He put an arm around Carrie's shoulders. "Me and Miss Carrie, we're old friends, did you know that?"

Carrie blushed and tried to smooth down the hair that stuck out from her braids. She knew she must look completely disheveled. Suddenly what Cody had said at first registered with her.

"Wait a minute. Did you say you're leaving the Pony Express?" she asked, incredulous.

"It wasn't just me that decided it. The telegraph closed down my home station and I thought, Billy, old pal, reckon it's time to be moving on. Hey now, don't look at me like that. I've been with the Pony from the start, you know. I've done my share of hard riding."

"It isn't that," Carrie mumbled.

"What? What's that?" Cody leaned towards her.

Carrie looked around at the faces of the men and blushed again. She looked up at Cody boldly. "Could we go outside and talk?" she asked.

"Course we can. As a matter of fact, you can walk with me out to my horse and let me know if you'd like me to

174

deliver any messages to your folks at the ranch. I'll be going right by there." He started towards the door.

Carrie followed him outside.

"So are there any messages you want me to pass along?" Cody asked.

"Yes, you can tell them all I miss them," Carrie said.

Cody waited. "Is that it?"

"That's all I can think of at the moment."

"Hey, what's the matter? You sound like you're mad at me or something." Cody looked puzzled.

Carrie turned away and looked off at the mountains, shrouded by storm clouds. It would rain soon, the beginning of the spring storms.

"Carrie? Come on, what is it?"

Don't you know what I'm getting at, you fool, Carrie thought. Now, if you'd just take me in your arms and hold me close and—Jack.

The name flew into her mind. Jack? What's he got to do with this? Not Jack, Billy. Billy, who was standing right here; Billy, only an arm's reach away; Billy, who was looking uncomfortable, like he wished he were anywhere but here. Uh, oh, Carrie thought, I've made a mistake. This is all wrong.

Suddenly she felt shy and sort of dumb. She tried to

think of something to say. "I don't know. I guess I'm sorry that you're leaving the Express. I used to think that if I got to be a rider that you and I would ride together someday."

Cody looked confused. "But Pony riders ride alone, you know that..." He stopped and the confusion was replaced with a look of understanding. He hesitated. His face reddened. "You know it's funny, but for all that you're such a pretty little thing, I guess I never noticed that you were a girl. You're so tough and ornery that I just sort of got accustomed to thinking of you like another fella. I'm sorry, I really am."

"Sorry for what? What did you think? That I...? Don't be silly, I never..." Carrie felt foolish for having begun the conversation. "I just meant that we would be equals once I was a rider and that the two best riders on the Express should ride together someday."

"Oh? Well, now I'm sorry all over again. I must think a lot of myself, huh?"

"You always did." Actually, it wasn't all that bad, Carrie thought, that Cody didn't share her feelings. She was not devastated by Cody's lack of interest. But shouldn't she be? A weight lifted from her heart.

"Hey, you know, with the reputation you have as a Pony rider, I'll bet the army would take you as a scout. What do you think? Then we could ride together," Cody said.

Carrie looked at him in disbelief. "Leave the Pony? Me? Now, when they need riders as much as ever? Never."

"It was just a thought, don't get riled." Cody chuckled. "Hey, would you like me to give Captain Slade your regards when I get to Fort Laramie?"

Carrie laughed. Cody *was* an amusing fellow. And that's all he was, she realized, an amusing friend and fellow Pony rider. She felt a great desire to go home. Home, where Jack Rising waited.

Seventeen

April came again, and Carrie thought how quickly the year had passed. It had been a year since the Pony Express had begun. The Express had been highly successful as far as its customers were concerned, she knew they were happy with the service rendered; it had certainly been far better than any stagecoach had been. But now it seemed everyone was eagerly looking forward to the telegraph and even greater speed with their news, now that war was just around the corner.

Adventuresome as it was, the Express had not turned out to be just what Carrie had imagined. A year had passed and, looking back, she hardly recognized the girl she had been then. She'd grown up this year.

The work was impossibly hard and she missed home and ranch life more than she'd ever thought possible. She found herself thinking about it, and about Jack Rising all the time. She'd managed to save most of her pay and with almost six hundred dollars, felt confident that she'd have enough to buy Outlaw when the time came. She looked forward to the day when she rode Outlaw home for good.

She came in one night, dragging herself to her bunk,

and was met with unwelcome news.

"Hey there, Sutton, aren't you going to eat?" Ben asked her.

Carrie shook her head, pulling off her boots, "I'm too tired. I just need to sleep for awhile."

"Reckon you best rest up as quick as you can. You've got to take over the Elwood Relay run come morning. This station's being shut down. Dang telegraph."

The words barely registered in Carrie's exhausted mind. "Can I take Outlaw?" was all she could say before dropping off to sleep. She heard Ben's answer as if from a dream.

"Reckon all the stock's going with you. Sure am going to miss you around here."

The next day Carrie, with Outlaw and four other Express ponies, was at Elwood Relay, twenty miles west of Cassidy Ranch. The day after that, Carrie stood beside a restless Outlaw getting last minute instructions from Tommy Walsh, station attendant. He was an older man, probably in his late fifties, sturdy and rough, and he obviously didn't care for the idea of a girl rider. It was drizzling cold rain and she was eager to be off.

Tommy was going over things he'd already told her a number of times.

"The trail is well marked. Just stick to it and you can't go wrong. You oughta make Grubs Wells by dusk, and you switch horses there. Then, go on to Log Station and the next rider'll take over." He looked at Outlaw and frowned. "You oughta be riding one of our regular ponies. This one ain't going to know the way."

Carrie looked at the man and tried to sound encouraging. "He's got an instinct, and he's the fastest horse the Express has got. I'll need the speed on a strange trail and in the rain. We'll make it all right."

Tommy just scowled, unconvinced. "Just remember what I told you. There's a pack of Sioux out fer trouble here 'bouts, so just be careful and keep an eye out."

"Outlaw can outrun any Indian pony there is."

"Just you and your pet horse get the mail through and don't be fooling around," he snapped.

Carrie had a sinking feeling that this was going to be a tough home station. "You don't approve of me, do you?" she asked straightforwardly.

Tommy met her eyes. "Can't say that I do. But it ain't for me to say. Just do as I tell you and you'll be at Log Station before supper." There was the sound of hooves on the road and shouting. "Here comes Blackie now. You ready?"

Carrie turned Outlaw so that he was facing the road west and smiled her most beguiling smile at Tommy. "I'm always ready."

The rider came dashing into the yard, almost crashing into Carrie and Outlaw before he pulled his lathered horse to a stop.

"It's war!" he shouted. "The Rebs fired on Fort Sumter! It's war!" He tossed the bags to Carrie, who caught them deftly and threw them onto her saddle.

"Spread the word down the line, Pony Gal, this country's going to war."

Carrie didn't take precious time to answer; she clicked her tongue at Outlaw, swinging into the saddle as he thundered away.

The trail to Grubbs Well was as Tommy had said, well marked. Although the drizzle turned into a full fledged spring rain, Carrie and Outlaw made good time. Knowing that she was carrying such important news spurred her on. War! She wasn't sure what this would mean to her personally, but she knew it was a historical day for the country. She thought about Anna and her family in Pennsylvania. Would they be involved in the war? What did it all mean?

The Grubbs Well station came into view and as she rode in, she did as Blackie had done, shouting out the news.

There was no one to hear her shouts, no one there wait-ing with a fresh mount and eager ears. The station, one of the many hastily built shacks and corrals put up by the Express, was deserted.

"Ho there! Hey, is anybody here?" she called out. She didn't know if she should dismount and look around or go ahead to Log Station. A hushed voice startled her. She pulled her gun from its holster and whirled around.

A man, gray-whiskered and slumped, emerged from be-hind some bushes. "Boy, over here," he whispered.

Carrie kept her gun leveled at him. "Who are you?" she asked. "Come on out from there. Don't try anything— I got my gun on you."

The man stepped forward, arms raised. "Whoa there, son, don't shoot. It's just me, Willy." Carrie saw then that he seemed to be a harmless old man and she lowered her pistol.

"Willy, you say?" Carrie jumped to the ground. "I ain't no boy. I'm Carrie Sutton, the Express rider. Where's ev-eryone else? Where's the horses?"

Willy's eyes lit up. "You're that girl rider? I heard of you."

Carrie thought it best to speak slowly and deliberately. "Willy, listen, I've got to get along in a hurry. Where's my horse?"

Willy pointed to Outlaw. "He's right there, ain't he?"

Carrie took a deep breath. "No, I mean where's my relief horse? Where are the horses that belong here at this station? Where are the other men?"

Willy shook his head sadly. "A rider came through here and told us there was gonna be an Injun raid, so Davy and Earl drove the horses off so's the Injuns wouldn't get 'em."

"What? All the horses?" Carrie said, unbelieving.

"Yup."

"And they left you here alone?"

"No, I stayed on my own." He grinned at her, showing a toothless mouth. "I reckoned I'd wait 'til the Injuns had done come and gone and then I'll mosey on in and fix me up some vittles."

Carrie put a hand on Outlaw's rain-soaked neck. "What about me?"

"You're welcome to join me, o'course," Willy said, oblivious of Carrie's predicament. "But them redskins ain't been here yet and we got to hide out 'til then. We can stay dry under those bushes there, but you'll have to run your horse off so's they don't get him."

Carrie gnashed her teeth in anger. "Why would the station men do such a fool thing? How could they know for sure that there would be a raid?"

Willie shrugged. "I don't know, but the man who came said he had orders from Slade himself. You gonna stay with me? I'd be plumb honored."

"No, Willy, I'll have to go on with Outlaw." She climbed back into the saddle, frustrated and angry. "How could they take all the horses? Didn't they know there was a rider coming in today?"

"In all the 'citement, I reckon they forgot." Willy shrugged again.

Carrie turned Outlaw back onto the trail and urged him into a gallop, leaving Willy and his slow wits quickly behind.

The ride to Log Station was another thirteen miles. Carrie hated having to push Outlaw so hard, but there was no helping it. The news she carried was more important than she or Outlaw.

She pondered what Willy had said about Slade's messenger. If what she and Jack suspected was true, then this was the sort of trouble she might have expected. She kept her gun out and ready.

She reached the next station just after dark. The cabin, larger and better built than the one at Grubbs Wells, was just as deserted. There were no lights and no sign of life as

Carrie rode in. The rain was beating down hard and Outlaw was wheezing with exertion.

Oh no, Carrie thought, I don't like this. She hoped maybe they were inside, avoiding the rain.

"Hello?" she called. "Anybody around? Where is everybody?"

The door to the cabin opened. She could see the gleam of a pair of eyes. Relief flooded through her.

"Hey, come out. I won't hurt you. Where's my relief rider? Where's the horses? I couldn't get a fresh mount at Grubbs and my horse is about to drop." The man remained in the dark doorway and Carrie felt impatient. "Will you come out of there and help me? Please?"

The door flew open and an Indian brave in full war paint jumped out at her, tomahawk raised. Outlaw reared, nearly knocking Carrie from the saddle. Carrie's scream mingled with the brave's whoop. As Outlaw reared, his front hooves slashed out at the Indian, forcing him back into the doorway. Carrie, collecting her wits, yanked on the reins, turning Outlaw towards the road, and they bounded away. Carrie rode in a blind panic, leaning over the stallion's neck, urging him forward with his last ounce of strength. She looked back over her shoulder, expecting to see the Indian in hot pursuit, but he wasn't there and she began to get herself, and her horse, under control.

"Whoa there, boy." She let his pace slow but left him in a canter. "Steady, Outlaw. We've got to go on, we've got no choice. We've got to make it. The next relay's on a ranch. If we can just get there, we'll be all right."

The rain poured down.

Eighteen

It was dark now and raining heavily as Outlaw sluggishly made his way through the mud. He was struggling, and Carrie leaned over his neck, cooing to him and coaxing him on. She was also trying to watch for the trail through the rain and dark. It was like going into an unfamiliar room with eyes closed. She thought she would have to dismount and lead Outlaw when she was suddenly pitched forward and over his head as he stumbled, floundering down the bank of a mud-filled gully.

Carrie landed on her back in the mud with a soft plop. She heard Outlaw sliding down the side and into the mud. He snorted in confusion and fear. Carrie groped her way through the darkness.

"Outlaw?" She whistled softly. "Where are you, boy?"

She could hear him, struggling to free himself from the mud. Carrie blindly followed the sounds and, crawling across the mud, finally reached him. She almost slid into the deep buffalo wallow where the stallion was trapped. He was up to his shoulders in the mud and too fatigued to fight his way out. His breath was labored. Carrie tried to soothe him, rubbing his neck, as tears of despair ran down her face.

"Dear God, help me," She prayed aloud. "What do I do now?" She was afraid to shout for help for fear that she'd bring the Indians. She was panting, frightened, trying to find some order in her chaotic mind. What would Jack do? she thought. That calmed her— thinking of Jack, thinking of anything other than this mess she was in.

"He'd do what he had to do— get this mail on its way to the next rider," she said, stroking Outlaw and trying to propel herself into action. The thought of leaving Outlaw alone in this mudhole brought fresh tears to her eyes. She made her way around to his side and took the mochila from the saddle. She began to cry.

"I've got to leave you here, fella. There's nothing else I can do. But I'll be back as soon as I can get some help." Carrie made an effort to pull herself together, shuddering as she tried to stifle her sobs. She wiped her teary eyes and runny nose with her sleeve, succeeding only in smearing mud across her face. "I've got to be strong now and do my job like you done yours. Don't be scared, Outlaw, I'll be back." She hoped the tone of her voice would reassure and soothe him and somehow get across to him the need to be calm and wait for her return.

She calculated the Simpson Ranch was about five or six

miles up the road. It might take her three or four hours to return with help. The image of Outlaw, alone, helpless and immobile, made her cry again. She laid her face against his and gave way to great heaving sobs before crawling to the bank and up the side.

It seemed to Carrie that it took an agonizingly long time to crawl, scraping along on her belly, like a snake, to get to the bank. She was covered with mud except for the streams of tears running down her cheeks and chin. She turned back once but couldn't see Outlaw now in the darkness. "I'll be back," she said to him, "I promise." He nickered in reply.

She went on; the mud that covered her and the mailbag was quickly washed away by the unceasing rain. She gripped the mochila tightly and could not stop crying. She gulped in air between sobs, falling over and over again in the mud, blinded by tears and darkness and rain.

A fire was beginning behind her eyes and her movements felt leadened. Her muscles ached, every step became an effort and yet stopping never entered her mind. The image of Outlaw, caught alone in the buffalo wallow in the pouring, chilling rain, sped her on. She kept carefully to the trail, squinting through the pain in her head.

The trail through the woods seemed endless. The rain

was a solid curtain all around her. After a while she could only hope that she was going in the right direction. Her throat was closing up and her whole body reverberated with aching fire.

Rational thought began to seep away. She started to believe that she was dreaming, that she was having a terrible nightmare. She thought that must be it because all of a sudden there were Indians among the trees.

Except they weren't really Indians, although they were dressed like Indians and wore feathers in their hair. These men were white. Streaks of brown ran down their bare arms and legs. Carrie, in her sick, bemused mind, thought they must be white men made up to look like Indians.

One of the white Indians came towards her. He held a long hunting knife above his head. Carrie closed her eyes, certain that she would shortly feel the knife cutting into her. She reached for her gun and was not surprised to find it gone. Wasn't that the way dreams always worked? If this were real, her gun was undoubtedly buried in the mud beside Outlaw, thrown from her hand in the fall.

But this was just a bad dream, of course, so Carrie gripped the mochila more tightly and kept on, walking straight towards the white Indian's knife.

The world began to swim before her eyes. The Indian

stood directly in front of her, knife raised, reaching to take the mailbag. Carrie, through the fever that was building in her, saw that the man was Pike. Then she knew it was not a dream. It was real and Pike was going to kill her and the mail would not go through and it would be her fault, her failure and worst of all, no one would find Outlaw before it was too late and he would die, too.

Then Pike's face, so near to hers, suddenly registered shock. He grunted and fell to the ground. A man stood over him and with her last moment of consciousness, Carrie reached out her hand in thanks and greeting.

"My Indian friend," she whispered and collapsed.

Nineteen

For a long time there was only a hot blackness and some-times voices, one voice in particular, cool and soothing, that matched the hands that stroked her forehead. Then she was able to see blurred faces and hear the voices more distinctly. After a while she recognized the hands which soothed her hot brow and the cool voice that murmured, softly comforting. Anna was with her.

As the blackness faded, Carrie had bad dreams— dreams of rain and a big, black and white stallion mired in mud, struggling to get free, weak whinnies, alone in the dark. Over and over again Carrie awakened herself, moaning and crying until Anna's worried face bent over her, and Carrie, seeing her, felt safe and able to sleep again.

Then one day she was there, really there, back in her own room. Things were in focus again; the fever was gone.

"Anna?"

"Carrie?" Anna was sitting by the window and, hearing Carrie, dropped her sewing and immediately came to her bedside. "Carrie, thank God. You're going to be all right."

"Outlaw?" She had to know.

"Don't try to talk now, honey." Anna smoothed the hair

back from Carrie's face, smiling down at her. "You're going to have to get your strength back. You've had pneumonia for over two weeks. We can talk about everything later."

Two weeks! How could that be? But Anna was right. Carrie could tell she had no strength. She felt weighed down and groggy. She could have easily fallen back into sleep, but she had to know about Outlaw. Where was he?

"Anna-" Her voice was like a croak.

"Carrie, please, not now. You rest and I'll bring you some soup and later we'll talk." Anna spoke quickly and brightly. "Hank and Jack have been haunting this room and they'll want to know that you're awake, that you're better and-"

"Anna," Carrie interrupted. "Please. Just one thing. Just tell me about Outlaw. Is he all right?"

Anna looked stricken and turned away and then Carrie knew. But she had to hear it, had to have it said aloud.

"Tell me, Anna."

Anna pulled the chair up next to the bed and took one of Carrie's hands. She didn't look at Carrie's face; she kept her eyes on the hand as she spoke.

"Some men from the Simpson Ranch went looking for him the next day, after word had been sent to us. As it was, Jack had a feeling something had happened and he'd gone to check on you. Anyway, you were delirious, and kept on about your horse being caught in some buffalo wallow." Anna paused and Carrie wrapped her fingers around Anna's hand, gripping it.

"They found him, Carrie, but he was dead, on the road. The men said it looked as though he had pulled himself from the mud—he must have— although the rain had washed him clean. The saddle was gone. They think the Indians took it. It just must have been too much for him. I'm so sorry, honey, I really am." The tears in Anna's eyes flowed over, dripping onto their tightly held hands.

Carrie stared at the ceiling. She'd been pretty sure what Anna was going to say and had prepared herself for the grief, but now she felt nothing. A numbness enveloped her. She closed her eyes, willing herself back into the black-ness, into the oblivion. Anna was right, she wasn't strong enough to hear this.

Later, Carrie was strong enough to grieve, and she did, in great, painful sobs. If only it had been some other way, if only he hadn't been all alone in the rain, if only she hadn't gotten sick, if only, if, if, if...

In spite of her grief, she grew stronger every day; her recovery was steady and rapid. Hank and Jack visited her room: Hank sat with her, holding her hands, obviously re-lieved and Jack tried to cheer her up. He also was able to fill her in on that night. She *had* seen Pike.

"It was Pike and some men of his, dressed and painted like Indians, who ran off the stock at the relay stations and terrorized the station keepers," Jack told her. "Pike's dead; he was found on the trail leading to the Simpson Ranch. Three of his men were nearby, tied to trees."

"What about Slade?" she asked.

"He's still around, I reckon. He's probably in his office at Fort Laramie. Pike's men told us all they knew and it wasn't much. They took their orders directly from Pike. There's no proof that Slade was involved, but I know different."

"So do I," Carrie said. She was beginning to remember that horrible night. The Indian whom she had saved from the wolves had saved her from the human wolves. He had carried her to the edge of the stable yard of the Simpson Ranch, which had been closer than she'd thought. She had watched the Indian make his silent way back to the woods. She had stumbled forward, toward the men who had been waiting for the Pony rider, and they had rushed to her just before she'd collapsed.

"You were able to mutter, 'It's war. Fort Sumter', before passing out, still clutching the mochila," Jack told her.

"You did yourself proud, girl," Hank said, pride shining

in his eyes. Or was it tears? "The mail went through and the important war message got delivered, thanks to you."

"Thanks to Outlaw, you mean," Carrie said.

Jack nodded. "He did give it his all. He had heart. But you, you managed to make it the rest of the way to the relay getting sicker and sicker the whole way. I don't know how you did it."

"I owe my life to the Indian," Carrie said. "Pike was going to kill me."

Hank took Carrie's pale hand in his grizzled one. He looked at her earnestly. "I wish I had that Indian here right now to thank him myself."

"Maybe you can someday," Jack said. "He's probably still around here, keeping a protective eye on Carrie. I hope so, anyway, as long as Slade is still loose." There was a rare seriousness to Jack. "Slade could be carrying a grudge."

Hank frowned. "What would ole Joe Slade have against Carrie?"

"I think Slade was trying to sabotage the mail deliveries for the sake of the Confederacy's secret society. He didn't want certain news to reach California. Like the news that war had been declared," Jack said.

"You know that for a fact?" Carrie asked, interest reviving her.

"Yes, I do. I've been in contact with a special agency which has been following the activities of some men they know are involved with this secret society from the south. I believe two of those men are the same ones Carrie happened upon in Box Elder last spring."

It all made sense to Carrie. "So you've known what's been going on, haven't you?"

Hank looked from one to the other, his puzzlement evident. "Has something been going on?" He focused on Jack and frowned. "Did you know Carrie could be in danger and you never let on?"

Jack shook his head. "I didn't know for certain until a few weeks ago. I was in town when the news came over the telegraph that Fort Sumter had been fired on and war was declared. It all fell into place. It occurred to me that Slade might already have received the news. That's when I went after Carrie. As it was, I would have been too late. But Carrie managed to get the news through anyway and she foiled every other attempt, too. I guess that would be enough to get Slade good and mad. I think we all know how Slade feels about killing."

"Yeah," Carrie said, "it's as natural to him as breathing."

"Someone oughta do something about him." Hank stood up. "I reckon I'll hitch up the wagon and ride on into Box Elder. I can use that new-fangled telegraph to send a message to the commander over at Fort Laramie to arrest ole Joe."

"You can't do that, Hank," Jack said, "We don't have any solid proof that Slade was involved. He's covered his tracks pretty good. I was thinking I'd go to the Fort and see what I can find; maybe he overlooked something."

"Well then, I'll go with you," Hank said.

"We can't both go; someone has to stay here and guard the women."

"I don't need guarding, Jack Rising," Carrie said, sitting up straighter.

Jack grinned. "She's getting her spirit back, Hank. I never thought I'd be so glad to hear that determined tone of voice."

"Well, hear this then: I'm going with you to Fort Laramie."

Jack shook his head. "No you're not."

"Why not? You might need my help. I'm not sick anymore." Carrie knew that it was Joe Slade's fault that Outlaw had died; he was responsible for running off the stock at the stations and for Pike almost killing her. If there was a way she could blame Slade for the rain storm that night, she'd do that, too. She wanted to see that he paid, and paid dearly, for his crimes. And for Outlaw's life.

"You ever hear of a relapse? I won't risk it, even if you would. If you try to get out of that bed to go with me I'll have Anna tie you to the bedposts. I swear I will," Jack warned.

Carrie shrugged and tried to look resigned, but she was thinking, I'm not much on warnings, Jack Rising; Hank could tell you that.

Twenty

Carrie smiled as she adjusted the blanket on her bed to make it look as if she were in it. I'm getting good at this, she thought.

She, with Anna and Hank, had watched Jack ride away a short time ago. It had been an effort to pretend to be resigned to staying home. Now she was supposed to be napping. Anna had left the house to work in the garden, so it was an easy matter to slip, unseen, from the house. Carrie stepped out onto the front porch. She knew Anna was at the back of the house, but where was Hank? There was nothing else to do but walk brazenly across the stable yard. No one stopped her. Carrie crept to the rear of the stable and eased open the back door, letting a stream of light into the shadowy interior. She drew in a sharp breath. In the flood of sunshine stood General, one of the ranch wagon horses, saddled and bridled. Hank held the reins.

"Hank? What? How did you...?"

"Don't you think, after all this time, I know you pretty good? You'd better get going or you'll never catch Jack."

"What about Anna?"

"I'll tell her later. I'll see that she understands. You get going and hurry on back. Here." He held out a gun.

Carrie took the pistol and slipped it in the waist of her pants. She wrapped her arms around Hank's wrinkled neck and hugged him tightly.

"Thank you, Hank." She released him and pulled back to look at his face. "I love you, Hank."

"I love you, too, Carrie."

Carrie turned to the waiting horse, shaking her head sadly. What she wouldn't give to have Outlaw right now. Don't think about that, she scolded herself. This old horse would have to do. She climbed into the saddle and took the reins.

"Good bye, Hank," she said. "Tell Anna I'll be fine. I'll be with Jack. We probably won't be gone long. Just long enough to bring old Slade to justice." She clicked her tongue to get General moving.

Once outside, Carrie kicked General into a canter. He snorted in indignation. "Sorry, old boy," Carrie said, "but we have to catch Jack."

She didn't have to go far to find him; he was waiting for her a mile up the road.

"I had a feeling you'd be along," he said.

"I reckon I can't fool anyone any more."

"Reckon not. How're you feeling?"

It didn't seem like it would be a good idea to tell Jack that her head ached with a constant throbbing. "I'm fine," she replied.

"All right then, let's go."

They started for Fort Laramie, Jack slowing Flag's pace to match General's.

"I think I've figured some more things out," Jack said. "For instance, I don't think there was ever any danger from the Indians in this area. I think Slade set the whole thing up, sending out his men made up to look like Indians, like the night they almost killed you. The Indian uprising last fall was the doing of the Paiutes in Nevada and Utah. Most of the tribes around here are Sioux; I heard that they went to Fort Laramie to smoke the peace pipe and negotiate a treaty. If anyone broke that treaty, it was Slade."

Carrie nodded. "And we know why he was doing it. He wanted to disrupt the Pony Express and blame it on the Indians." She paused, remembering. "Or on road agents."

"That's right. And why? Because he had made some rotten deal with the people who were trying to get California on the side of the Confederacy."

"I'd have thought that Slade's loyalties would be with the North," Carrie said.

"His loyalties are with the almighty dollar," Jack replied.

"You can bet they were paying him plenty. We have to find something that will tie him in with Pike and everything that happened. If we don't, he'll be getting away with it."

"Are you sure he's still going to be at Fort Laramie? He could be long gone by now."

Jack shrugged. "He may be gone, but his office will still be there and there's a chance he left some clue behind. Besides seeing Slade behind bars, I'd like to see the Indians vindicated. They don't deserve the reputation Slade's given them."

"You're a good man," Carrie said.

"Yes, I know. It's the cross I have to bear," he said lightly, not looking at her. "I think I'd rather be a flashy, self-centered hero; people seem to like them more."

"What people?" It seemed to Carrie that there was something unspoken beneath the light tone.

"Oh, never mind." Jack smiled. "Do you think you could persuade that mule you're riding to plod along a little faster? At this rate we'll be lucky to get to the fort before the war's over."

They rode all day and into a moonless night. Carrie was glad when Jack suggested stopping for the night. General's uneven gait was causing her head to pound, but she endured it uncomplainingly. She was sure if she mentioned it Jack would turn back for home immediately, and that would never do. She would endure anything if it meant a chance at capturing Slade.

Jack made a sort of stew from the meat, potatoes and carrots he'd brought.

"You have hidden talents, Jack. How did you learn to cook?"

Jack laughed. "Anyone can cook a simple stew."

"Not me. That was one thing my Pa could never teach me. He and Hank always did the cooking." Carrie spooned the last of the stew into her mouth and sighed with pleasure. Food never tasted as good as it did after a full day's riding.

"You'd better learn to cook someday. Or you may never catch a husband," Jack chuckled.

Carrie looked at him, startled. "I don't want a husband." She'd never thought about having one before. She'd never even thought of Bill Cody in that way.

"You may want to get married one day. Although, I guess any man who hitches up with you won't be doing it for your cooking."

"What's that supposed to mean?"

"I mean that you're so pretty, especially now, in the light

of the campfire." He looked at her critically. "You're thinner, and much paler since your illness. But it flatters you. You'd turn heads everywhere you went if you could stay clean and if you wore more conventional clothing."

Carrie lowered her head and fed wood into the fire. She was blushing deeply; her face felt hot and she knew it wasn't because of the proximity of the fire. It was the nearness of Jack Rising. Something in the nearness was causing her heart to beat wildly in her chest. She looked up and their eyes met and held. Flames, reflected from the fire, were leaping in Jack's eyes, seemingly with a life of their own. Carrie felt as if she were caught in a summer storm; thunder rumbled in her head and a bolt of lightning sent tingles through every nerve in her body. She quickly bent her head again, confused and suddenly scared. "It'll be summer again soon," she said after a few moments. She wondered if Jack heard the quiver in her voice.

"That it will," Jack replied easily.

Something had passed between them, something strong and undeniable, but something that could be let go of for now. There would be time for them, that Carrie knew. And she could tell Jack knew it, too.

"Let's get some shuteye," he said, standing and stretching. "We'll get started at first light."

They laid out their bedrolls on opposite sides of the fire. Carrie got as close as she could to the fire; the nights were cold. She couldn't fall asleep right away, but lay there thinking. She thought about Jack: what a good friend he was, how he had come to know her so well and—she had to admit it—how important he was to her. Had she ever told him that? He never made a secret of caring for her; he had shown it in so many ways. Happiness seemed to wash over her. When this journey was over, she would confess her feelings for him. First, however, they needed to concentrate on capturing Slade and then... well, there would be time to tell him. And she would. She fell asleep smiling peacefully.

She was riding Outlaw and they were flying high in the sky, heading for Fort Laramie to catch Joe Slade. She thought Cody was riding alongside her, but when she looked it was Jack. Oh, that made her so happy. She didn't care if she never saw Cody again; it was so wonderful to be with Jack.

"Jack!" she called. He didn't seem to hear her against the rushing wind. She urged Outlaw on faster and came up beside him. She reached out and touched his arm. "Jack? Jack, I care about you. I really do. I love you."

He turned to her, his eyes a darker blue than she had

ever seen them. "I know, Carrie. You never wanted that fool Cody, did you? It was me all along." He smiled at her and his teeth glistened brightly. His smiled widened and his teeth began to glare in their brightness, blinding her. She raised her arm to cover her eyes, yet still they burned from the intensity of Jack's smile.

"Carrie?"

Her eyes flew open. She was lying on the ground on a blanket. It was dawn, very cool and damp. Jack was crouched near her.

"Hey, come on, sleepyhead. Let's get a move on. What's the matter? You're looking at me kind of strange."

Carrie rubbed her eyes, willing herself into wakefulness. "I was dreaming. You woke me up, that's all." Her eyes were still burning and Carrie could tell she was getting sick again. Her head was starting to ache.

Jack stood and looked down at her. "Are you all right? Let me feel your forehead. I told you you shouldn't have come."

As he bent to put his head on her forehead, Carrie's dream came back to her and she sat up, brushing his hand aside. "You think you know everything, don't you, Jack Rising?"

Jack looked startled. "No, not everything, I suppose. You

are looking flushed."

"I'm all right! Really." She didn't know why she felt angry with him. It was her dream, of course, Jack's reaction to her confession of love. Would he be that arrogant in reality? Carrie doubted it and yet the dream left her feeling unsure of herself.

They didn't reach Fort Laramie until well after dark that night. Carrie led Jack to the livery stable where they watered, fed and rubbed down the horses. It was an effort for Carrie; her head hurt and her muscles ached. She wasn't going to tell Jack just to hear him say I told you so and have him send her to the army infirmary. If only she could rest for awhile.

"Let's get some sleep now." Jack said, "We really can't do much until daylight, anyway."

Bless you, Jack, Carrie thought.

They slept late the next morning and were awakened when the livery keeper came in to feed the horses. The long night of sleep did Carrie a world of good. She felt much better, ready to take on a dozen Slades.

No one answered their knocks at The Overland Pony Express Office. The door was unlocked, so they went inside. The office was apparently still being used; papers were stacked neatly on the desk with several journals, a coat was draped across a chair, and a plate of food, half eaten, had been set aside on a corner table. Slade must still be around.

"Let's get to work," Jack said. "Slade could come back anytime." He began to look through the journals.

"Where should I look?"

Jack made a sweeping motion with his hand. "Look everywhere. Maybe we can find whatever was used to darken those mens' skin or maybe there'll be a letter from the southerners. Maybe there's a hidden cache of money. If Slade made a mistake we've got to find it."

Carrie began to search. She flipped through the pages of books, rifled through Slade's jacket pockets, went through the desk drawers. Every time there were footsteps outside she froze, expecting Slade to burst in on them. When the footsteps faded she and Jack returned to their efforts with renewed frenzy. The office was small and uncluttered. It didn't take long to finish the search.

"Well?" Jack asked.

"Nothing," Carrie replied in disgust. "Now what?"

"I don't know." Jack surveyed the room. "There's not much in the way of hiding places. Slade is either extremely tidy or extremely prepared for a quick get away."

Carrie's shoulders slumped. "He's beaten us. He's used

the Pony for his own gain, ruined the good reputation of honest Indians, and been responsible for death and destruction. And we know it and there's nothing we can do." She began to pace the room angrily. It was so unfair. Her hands curled into fists.

If Slade were here right now she probably wouldn't be able to stop herself from pummeling his smug face.

Her boots pounded the wood floor as she marched from one end to the other, feeling helpless and hating it. The sight of Jack, his eyes on her feet, his head cocked in a listening attitude, made her stop.

"What are you doing, Jack? You look like a hound that's been mule-kicked in the head."

Jack looked up excitedly. "Would you stomp across the room again?"

"What?"

"I could swear I heard the creak of a loose floor board and I just thought—"

"Under the floor boards, of course!" Carrie stamped her foot, walked a pace and stamped again. On the third stamp she felt a board shift.

"Here's the loose board."

Jack joined her and tested the floor with the heel of his boot. He got on his knees and examined it.

"Yep, this is it," he said. "Hand me the knife off that plate." He took the knife from Carrie and pried the board up. It lifted easily.

"What is it? What's under there?" Carrie danced in anticipation, glancing out the window nervously. "Hurry, Jack."

"It's a good thing you get riled so easily." He pulled something from the floor and triumphantly held it up for Carrie to see.

"My practice mochila!" The last time she'd seen the mailbag that Hank had made for her was when she'd thrown it at the head of the road agent on the trail to Deer Creek station.

"There's no doubt now that Slade was involved in that robbery attempt last November," Jack said. "This ties him in with Pike."

"Let's go tell Colonel Upson!" Carrie couldn't wait to see Slade's face when he was arrested.

"You run and get the Colonel. I can't run, I move too slow. I'm going to stay here in case Slade comes back. After all this, we don't want him to make an escape."

"Be careful."

Jack smiled into Carrie's worried face. "I have a gun and I know how to use it." He pushed her toward the door.

"Now go. Quick."

Carrie ran to the fort's headquarters. Colonel Upson was just coming out.

"Colonel Upson!"

He stopped and looked at her, puzzled. Then a look of recognition crossed his face and he smiled hesitantly. "Miss Sutton, what are you—"

"You have to come with me. There's no time to explain. Slade could still get away."

"Slade? Captain Slade?"

"Yes. I'll explain everything, but please hurry." She trotted on ahead of him. The Colonel motioned to several soldiers to follow.

It seemed to Carrie that it was an eternity before the Express office came into view. Jack was on the steps. He saw her and waved the mochila above his head, laughing. They were going to get Slade! Carrie waved back.

A movement behind Jack stopped her in her tracks. Slade stepped from behind the building, a gun in his hand, leveled at Jack.

"Jack!" Carrie screamed, and without thinking about it, reached for her gun, brought it up, and fired.

Twenty-One

The pistol jerked in Carrie's hand. A second later blood was spurting from a hole in Slade's shoulder and his gun lay useless at his feet. It had happened so quickly that Jack hadn't moved from his place on the steps. His eyes were wide with surprise.

"Get him, men," Colonel Upson ordered. Slade was surrounded before he could pick up his gun. He was clutching at his shoulder and glaring at Carrie. Carrie didn't flinch from his look but stared back, her chin held high.

"I told you I was a dead shot, Captain," she said. "I could have killed you. I reckon I have more mercy than you ever did."

Jack came and stood next to her. He handed the mochila to Colonel Upson. "This is proof that Slade was behind the near robbery of the mail delivery last November. We're certain he was also involved in all the supposed Indian raids and anything else that's disrupted the Express this past year."

"That's not proof of anything!" Slade snarled, his eyes blazing with fury. He stepped forward defiantly. "I haven't disrupted or raided a thing. You have no right to hold me,

Colonel."

"I don't understand any of this. I want a full explanation from the two of you," Colonel Upson said to Carrie and Jack. He turned to Slade. "I don't know what sort of thing you're involved in, Captain; I don't know for certain that it's anything at all. But I saw you try to shoot this young man. I think I'd better keep my eye on you until we get to the bottom of this. Men, take him to the doctor."

"You!" Suddenly Slade lunged at Carrie. He let go of his shoulder and reached for Carrie with both hands. He was grotesque as he came at her; his face was contorted with rage and hatred, one hand dripping blood. Carrie stood, transfixed, as his hands came within inches of closing around her throat. Then he was being pulled away and Jack was blocking her protectively, his arms drawing her close to him.

Slade struggled with the soldiers. "A foolish little girl and a cripple! How can you believe what they say? I'm the Express division agent. I am the law here! I am the law!" The men, with Slade being dragged along between them, marched off.

Colonel Upson shook his head as he watched them leave. "I'll wait for you in my office," he told Carrie and Jack, and walked away, leaving them alone.

"Are you all right, Carrie?" Jack asked softly.

"I'm fine," Carrie replied. I'd be fine forever, she thought, if I could just stay here in your arms.

"That was good shooting," Jack said. "You saved my life. I don't know what to say, except, thank you."

"I couldn't let that low down varmint shoot you, could I?" Carrie looked up at him and beamed a smile. She was trying to ignore the pain that was starting in her head again.

Jack returned her smile and moved apart from her a bit, taking her hands in his and looking in her eyes. "You're really something, Carrie." His smile faded. "Are you all right? Your hands are shaking."

Carrie withdrew her hands. "It's the excitement, I guess. Let's go on over to the Colonel's office and explain everything and then head for home. You know Hank and Anna aren't going to stop worrying until we get there."

"That sounds like a good idea." He casually put his arm around her shoulders as they walked. "You're sure you're all right?"

She tried to smile reassuringly. "Yes, I'm sure."

But she wasn't all right, not at all. Her head was pounding and she could feel herself shudder. She was having the relapse Jack had warned her about.

They were well on their way home, riding side by side,

when Carrie nearly fainted, swaying in the saddle. Jack's strong, capable hands stopped her from falling. He guided Flag close beside General and lifted Carrie, pulling her onto his saddle. She could feel his heart hammering in his chest and felt his breath against her neck. She let herself fall against him, feeling safe in his arms.

After that she rode on Flag with Jack, in the front of his saddle. He pushed his mare as fast as she could go, practically dragging the reluctant General with them. Carrie was beyond caring. She leaned back against Jack drowsily, feeling the fever building. She was very sick by the time they reached the ranch.

Weeks passed while Carrie recuperated. Then summer came, bringing warmth and sunshine and Carrie began to regain her old strength. She wasn't quite as robust, but she was improving. Her mental health was slower in coming back; she could hardly face the realization that Outlaw was gone. She stayed in a lot; hating to face the emptiness of the stable and corral. She knew Hank and Jack were making plans for the ranch, but she didn't join in. For right now, she didn't much care about anything.

She was sitting in her room, contemplating her future, when Anna came to the door.

"Carrie? Could you come out? There's someone here to

see you."

Carrie shrugged and followed Anna to the kitchen. Bill Cody sat at the table, a steaming cup of tea in front of him, grinning widely.

"Howdy, Pony rider," he said.

"Bill Cody? I thought you'd gone off to war by now." Her palms didn't sweat at the sight of him, nor did her heart do cartwheels. Cody smiled his most day-brightening smile. It was like looking on the face of a dear old friend, she realized. "I am heading for the fighting the day after tomorrow. I'm going to be a scout for the Union army. I've been doing some scouting and buffalo hunting for the army out here. I'm getting quite a reputation as a buffalo hunter, you know. I'm being called 'Buffalo Bill' all the time now." He seemed to swell with pride. Carrie wondered that she'd never seen what a braggart he was.

"But what are you doing here?" she asked.

A cloud seemed to pass over Cody's face, dimming his smile. "I was over at Fort Brigider and I heard tell of your misfortune and I came to see how you were getting on. I'm glad you're over your illness. Heard you were pretty sick."

Carrie was surprised by how much Cody seemed to know about her. "How'd you hear about me all the way at

Brigider?"

"Oh, you're the talk of the western territories. You're a hero, you know," Cody said, with a trace of pride in his voice.

"I am?" This was news to her.

Cody slapped his leg emphatically. "Shoot, yeah! I was proud to call you a friend of mine. You're quite a gal, Carrie Sutton. I admire you."

"You admire me?'

"Sure I do, and so do a lot of others, after what you did. Joe Slade wasn't too well liked, you know."

Carrie shook her head. "Jack was the one who figured out what was going on. He was the one responsible for catching Slade."

Cody shrugged. "You had a hand in it, too. You could go on being a Pony rider, you know."

Carrie opened her mouth to protest and he raised his palm to stop her.

"Now hear me out," he continued. "The telegraph's about taken over the Express now. It's just a matter of months before the Express is over. The end lines are all the way to Salt Lake City and Mountain View in Nevada. The glorious run of the Overland Pony Express has just about ended, but Wells Fargo is using Pony couriers to get the mail into all the new mining districts that are springing up all over the West. And, you wouldn't need no recommending letter from me to get hired on."

Carrie smiled. "As if the last one did any good. But anyway, I couldn't. I don't want to anymore."

"But why not? The riding wouldn't be as hard and the days wouldn't be as long and-"

"I just don't feel like it anymore," Carrie insisted.

Cody looked at her. "Is it because of that horse you lost? I heard about that, too."

Carrie nodded. "He was the best. He kept going and going and you know why? For me, because I asked him to. He would've done anything for me and I let him die." Carrie buried her face in her hands.

"Hey, hey." Cody, stricken-faced, went around the table to Carrie. "I know how it is to lose a good pony. And it's tough to have to go on, but there are other ones, good ones. You'll get another horse that you'll care as much about. I did and I didn't think I would."

Carrie shook her head. "There won't be another like Outlaw. I was going to buy him from the Express with my earnings. Now it's too late."

Words flooded out of Carrie, spilling over each other. "He was big. He could outrun anything with four legs and that ain't bragging; that's fact. He had a real broad chest, see, for power and he had legs that were just built for running. And he was beautiful, perfectly formed, with a long mane and tail. He was black and white, the shiniest black and the snowiest white you've ever seen. I used to brush him 'til he shone like velvet. He used to come when I whistled." Carrie paused, remembering.

"I don't know how I'm going to get along without him," she concluded, sighing. "But I'm done being a mail rider, I'm sure of that. I'm going to be a rancher now and stay settled, I guess."

Cody grinned. "I sure can't see that. You won't consider being a rider again?"

"No, that's one thing I know for certain. You were right all along, you know, it was a hard life."

They turned as Anna entered from outside.

"We're about to have lunch, Mr. Cody. Would you care to join us?" she asked.

Cody gave Anna a slight bow. "I'd be honored," he said grandly.

During lunch Cody spoke of what he would be doing for the army and how exciting it was going to be. Carrie couldn't help wondering what Jack was thinking. Did he feel that he was unable to go to war or work as a scout or hunter? It seemed to Carrie that Jack must be feeling left behind, and having been a girl all her life, Carrie knew the feeling. Then Cody turned his attentions to Jack, telling him that, limp and all, he would be welcomed into the army. Cody was effusive, telling Jack he was welcome to ride with him to Fort Laramie and sign up there if he wanted to.

"I don't think so," Jack said. "I'm going to give ranching a try."

Cody looked from Jack to Carrie. "Oh, I see how it is."

Carrie could feel her face flush. She stole a glance at Jack. He seemed to be blushing, too. Was he staying here because of her? And if so, what did that mean? It suddenly came to her with bright clarity that if Jack were to go away, if she were to lose him, too, she couldn't bear it.

The men were moving their chairs back, laughing and talking, but her mind was such a whirl she couldn't concentrate on what they were saying.

Cody bent over her and took her hands in his. "Goodbye now, Pony Gal," he said. "I don't know if we'll ever meet up again, but it's been my honor and pleasure to have known you. Take care of yourself." He turned to Jack, putting his hand out. "You take care of her, too."

Jack laughed. "Generally, she takes care of me."

Carrie looked up at him, startled. Did he really think that? But Jack was as much of a man as any she'd ever known. As much of a man as her Pa. He certainly didn't need her to look after him. He was joking, of course. Jack always joked. Her thoughts were so confused. Anna sat down and put a hand cautiously on Carrie's. "Are you feeling all right?" she asked.

"I feel fine, really. Tired, I guess." Carrie stood. "I think I'll go lie down." But she couldn't move. Feelings that had laid buried for so long rushed forward. The loss of her father, the anger she'd felt that he had left her, the feeling that she had let Outlaw down, that there was something she should have done, all the pain of growing up in the past year...

Anna got up and put her arms around Carrie slowly, as if expecting Carrie to shake them off at any moment, and held her in a tight hug.

Carrie allowed it for a moment, leaning awkwardly against Anna. She started to pull away but Anna held her tight.

Anna whispered, "It's all right, Carrie." Carrie dissolved against her, wrapping her arms around Anna and sobbing on her shoulder. And suddenly she felt as though it was going to be all right.

Twenty-Two

"I didn't think I'd be able to get along without Outlaw. He was all I had those last weeks on the Express. You know what? I used to go out to the stable and talk to him. I'd be so tired, but more than that, I was so lonely that I couldn't sleep. I had to talk to someone; someone I was sure would understand what I was feeling. So I'd talk to him. And he'd listen, he did! He was my best friend.

"I really didn't think, after I woke up from the fever and realized Outlaw was gone, that I could go on without him. But I will, of course. I have to. Just like I had to go on without Pa. But, Hank," Carrie stopped and reached out to hold the old man's hands. "It would be too, too much if anything were to happen to you."

Hank patted her hand affectionately. "I ain't going nowheres for a long time, Carrie," he assured her. "After I am gone, though, there'll still be Jack."

"Jack." Carrie repeated. She couldn't be sure of Jack. She hardly knew him, really. He cared for her, Carrie thought. But, how much? He had tried to get to her that fateful night, had known Slade and his men would be after her and Carrie had a feeling he would have risked his life to save hers. Carrie leaned against the side of the stall, the third stall on the right, Outlaw's empty stall, and held back her tears. If only Jack had come a little sooner. If only it hadn't been raining. More "if's", as if they mattered. What was done was done. Jack had tried, that's what was important.

"You going off in a blue devil, girl? You're awful quiet all of a sudden." Hank sat on a crate in a corner of the stall, chewing a piece of hay and watching her. Even in the gloom of the stable Carrie could see the concern in his eyes.

"No, I'm all right, Hank." Carrie smiled to reassure him. "I was thinking how things change. I wanted so much to be a Pony Express rider. I was so stubborn, wasn't I? I guess I wanted to prove something."

"I reckon you did, at that."

"Yes, I did. I just wonder if it was worth it. Last year, when the Express started, I was such a little girl. Now I feel so much older and wiser." Carrie could see Hank's mouth was twitching itself into a grin. "What's so funny? Don't you think I've grown up this year?"

"Yep, I reckon you have." Hank allowed himself the grin. "But that stubborn, willful girl is still there."

Carrie lifted her chin, ready to protest, and then had to

relent, laughing.

Hank laughed with her. "There's plenty of time for growing up, Carrie. I reckon you are turning into one mighty fine woman. Your Pa would've been proud of you."

Hank rose and crossed the stall. As he stood in front of her, smiling fondly, Carrie thought, I have grown up in one way. Why, I'm as tall as Hank!

The past year had had a telling effect on her body, Carrie knew. She had curves now. She did not feel as gangly as she use to, there was a new gracefulness to her movements. She felt as though she had grown into her body. Sometimes, taking Jack unawares, she would catch him watching her and by the look in this eyes, knew that he approved of her appearance.

Apparently, Anna had also noticed Jack's attention.

"Carrie, how can I go home with a calm mind knowing that I'm leaving you here alone with—" Anna hesitated. "Well, with four men and no one to look after you properly?"

Carrie chuckled. "I'd hardly call Jack's little brothers 'men', and I know you can't be concerned about Hank. So that leaves Jack. Well, don't worry. Haven't I proven that I don't need someone to 'look after me'? If it turns out I do, Hank will be here."

The worry lines on Anna's brow did not ease. "I don't think you understand how inappropriate it is for a girl your age to be living alone with men. It simply isn't done."

Carrie had to smile. Anna had known her, and lived with her, for the better part of four years and still the woman seemed to hardly know her. To impose her morals on her was funny, Carrie thought. Still, Anna was the closest thing to a mother she would ever have and she didn't want to push her away as she used to.

Carrie looked around the tidy kitchen where they sat. The afternoon sunshine was streaming through the sparkling windows and splashing off a floor so clean you could eat from it. After Anna was gone would this room, or any room in this house, ever be so neat? Carrie didn't think so. Anna had gotten up and gone to the stove for more hot tea water and watching her putter around with teapot and kettle, Carrie felt a lump rise in her throat. She was going to miss Anna, whose presence had become comforting and routine.

"Anna, are you sure you really want to leave? There's a war starting back there, you know. Maybe you'd be better off staying here with us."

Anna turned back to Carrie, a smile lighting her face. "Oh, you don't know what it means to me to hear you say that, honey," she said. The smile faded a bit. "But I have to go. I need to see my parents, they're quite old now, and they may need me during this war. My sisters all have their own families to worry about." She returned to the table and sat down. "Now, what am I going to do about you?"

"Anna, please, everything will be all right, believe me. You know Jack. He's about the most trustworthy fella you could meet. And Hank will be keeping an eagle eye on me, you can count on that."

Anna nodded. "I suppose so."

"Anna," Carrie paused, swallowing the lump that had returned to her throat. "I know I've been awful to you and I want you to know how sorry I am. I'm sorry I didn't get to know you sooner. And, Anna, I'm going to miss you."

A tear made its way down Anna's cheek. "I always understood why you felt the way you did about me. I never held it against you. I'm glad we can finally be friends. And I'm going to miss you, too. So very much."

Carrie smiled. She could almost feel her Pa's approval in the room. You were right to marry her, Pa, Carrie thought, and I'm glad you did.

Carrie was especially glad the next day to know that Anna was there to talk to, because saying good-bye to Jack, even temporarily, was harder than she had imagined.

"I'll be back, Carrie, you can count on it," Jack told her. "Can't you believe me?"

"I'm scared, Jack. I lost my Pa and I've lost Outlaw and I'm scared to death I'm going to lose you, too."

"I didn't know you cared so much." He was teasing her but somehow it felt to Carrie that he was testing her, too.

She looked him straight in his sky blue eyes. The look in those eyes told her a lot of things, the least of which was that he did have every intention of returning. To her.

"I do care, Jack, I really do. Why can't your brothers find their own way out to our ranch?"

"I'm only going to Fort Laramie. Mark and Jimmy are young and they haven't traveled. I want to meet their stage and ride with them out here. You can understand that, can't you? I'll only be gone about a week. And when I get back, it'll be for good. You know that, don't you?"

Carrie didn't feel like being understanding. "Fine, then go." She turned her back.

He stepped up behind her, putting his hands on her shoulders to turn her towards him. He wrapped his arms around her and bent his face to hers. Their lips met, tentatively at first and then desperately. Carrie felt herself sinking into a whirlpool of sensation. Nothing in her life had prepared her for this moment. A moment that ended too quickly. It seemed as if they stayed like that for too short a time, their hearts beating together. And when Jack released her and stepped away, Carrie thought hers would break.

The days passed with excruciating slowness. Carrie tried to keep busy, hoping to force the hours to pass more quickly. She helped Hank with the ranch chores and Anna with her packing. Still, it seemed she couldn't stay busy enough to keep from thinking about Jack constantly.

Then the week was gone. Jack had said he'd be back in a week and there was no sign of him. Carrie didn't want to imagine all of the things that could happen to a lone rider on western trails. Her heart became a cold, hard stone in her chest. She missed him so much— his teasing, his laughter and their talks. And more.

She was well now, back to her old self. Except she wasn't the same. She was sixteen now, soon to be seventeen— a woman. She felt confused. Life seemed upside down to her. Her nights were uneasy, her sleep fitful.

It was a night after Jack had been gone a full two weeks, That Carrie had the dream.

She was walking across the deserted stableyard. There seemed to be no one left on the ranch but her, even their few head of cattle were gone from the fields. Somehow, though, she didn't feel quite alone. She was walking towards the corral purposely. She went to the gate, opened it, whistled and waited. Suddenly there he was— Outlaw! He was as big and beautiful as she remembered him. She felt engulfed in joy. She whistled again and he came to her, lowering his head to nuzzle her neck. She ran her hands eagerly over him, feeling his muscles quiver at her touch.

"Outlaw, Outlaw, you're alive. You beautiful thing, you're too ornery to die, aren't you? You're too strong to let some old buffalo wallow get the best of you. I should have known. I never should have doubted."

Grabbing a handful of his mane, Carrie leapt onto his back. He moved immediately, instinctively. She had only to barely put her heels to his flanks and he was off, running as he'd never run before. She clung to him, feeling the wind in her face, her heart singing with happiness. They became airborne and she laughed aloud with pure exhilaration.

Below her, the farm was no longer deserted; the fields were thick with cattle and horses, chickens ran squawking around the yard, pigs squealed happily in their muddy pens. Hank ambled out from the stable and waved up at her. Carrie waved back and with a slight pressure of her knees, turned Outlaw around to return. They glided downward, landing in the field among the fat cows and their calves.

"What beautiful stock we have," Carrie thought. "This is the ranch Pa always knew it could be." Carrie bent forward and draped her arms around Outlaw's neck, burying her face in his mane.

"Hey, Carrie," a familiar voice called.

Carrie looked up to see Jack standing at the fence. There were two teenaged boys with him and they looked so similar to him, she knew they must be his brothers. She slid from Outlaw's back but stayed in the field, savoring the moment. The sun was shining above while a cool breeze riffled her hair. The fields were green and dotted with cattle and horses as far as the eye could see. Outlaw stood nearby, grazing peacefully, his tail swishing with a soft sound. Jack waited patiently, his whole being smiling at her. Tears of joy ran down her face.

When Carrie woke her face was wet with real tears. This dream was different from any other. It did not leave her feeling empty or unfulfilled. She woke with a feeling of hope and anticipation.

As quickly as she could she pulled her clothes on and left the house. She needed to breath the moist air of dawn and think about her strange dream.

Soon Carrie was sitting in her favorite place, beneath the leafy birch trees, on the knoll above the ranch, beside her father's grave.

"You weren't in my dream this time, Pa," she said aloud. "But somehow you were, at the same time. Your ranch, the way you'd always planned it, was there, though. It's going to be Jack who will make that dream come true for you, I know it. For both of us. I wish he'd hurry up and get back here. The awful thing is, Pa, that I think I love Jack Rising. Isn't that crazy? Well, maybe not so crazy if you knew Jack. You would have liked him, Pa. He's like you in a lot of ways, but mostly he's himself. I thought for so long that I was in love with Bill Cody, but that was a silly girlish dream. Cody looked on me like another one of the fellas, or a little sister at best. But not Jack. He's my friend, probably the best one I'll ever have, including Hank. Jack understands me like no one else, except for Outlaw, in his own way. There's Anna and Hank and I do love them, but they're so different from me. Hank's so old and Anna's so refined. Oh well." Carrie sighed, looking down over the ranch and fields and the road that could go to Fort Laramie or Sweetwater.

Anna was in the house, probably awake by now, doubtless doing all the last minute things that needed doing before she left and Hank was in the stable, fixing tack or attending to any of the endless tasks necessary to the running of the ranch.

Carrie turned her attention to the road, looking at the whole valley. This is the most beautiful spot on earth, she thought. She had a wonderful view of the road in both directions. There was a steady stream of wagons heading west and farmers and ranchers heading into Box Elder. She watched men on horseback, riding alone or in pairs, some with small herds of cattle or horses, making their way to their own ranches or farms. There came some now, a fine lot of cattle from what she could see. They were being herded by three men.

Suddenly Carrie was on her feet, hand shading her eyes, looking as hard as she could, her heart pounding in her chest.

She raced down the hill and into the stable yard, shouting and panting. Anna and Hank came running.

"Jack's coming," she gasped "And he has—"

They rode into the yard whooping and hollering. Carrie was amazed to find that she recognized Jack's brothers from her dream. And these cattle— could they be the beginnings of all the stock she'd dreamt?

Hank directed the boys to get the herd through the gate and into the field and Anna stood among the swirling dust, laughing.

"Jack, what is all this?" Anna called above the boys' cries and the bawling of the cattle.

Jack eased himself from the saddle, rubbing his sore leg, but smiling so widely his face might have split.

"I'm sorry we took so long to get back but, as you can see, something came up to delay us," Jack replied, with obvious delight. "We met up with a family who'd been on their way west but decided to turn back. They changed their minds, can you believe it? Anyway, I couldn't pass up the offer they were making for this stock."

Jack's brothers had dismounted and stood shyly nearby. They were in their early teens, from the look of them. Jack motioned them forward.

"I want you all to meet my little brothers. This is Mark and this is Jimmy. Mark, Jimmy, this is Mrs. Sutton."

"Please call me Anna. It's so nice to finally meet you." Anna shook their dirty hands, smiling.

"This is Hank, boys. He'll be your boss, so you do what he tells you."

Hank shook their hands briskly. The boys were looking at him with respect and it was apparent Hank was enjoying it. "How do, fellas," he said.

Jack turned to Carrie, standing quietly a little way from the group. "And this," Jack said, "is Miss Carrie Sutton, famed Pony rider and hero of the west."

They boys turned to Carrie, their eyes wide.

"Jack Rising, stop it." Carrie put her hand out to the boys. "I'm just plain old Carrie. I feel like I've already met you two."

The older boy, Mark, cleared his throat. "We kind of feel like we know you, too, the way Jack goes on and on about you."

"Mark," Jack said, a threat in his voice.

"He does, Miss Carrie," Jimmy piped in. "We know all about you."

Jack put his hand over Jimmy's mouth, smiling sheepishly. "All right, boys, that's enough. Why don't you let Hank show you the bunkhouse? Will you do that, Hank?" Mark and Jimmy laughed as they allowed Hank to lead them away.

Carrie came and stood next to Jack. "So you've been talking about me, huh? Saying good things, I trust."

"Now why would I do that?"

Carrie laughed at his teasing tone. It felt so good to be hearing it again. "Come on, admit it. You missed me."

"Me, miss you?" Jack's arm circled Carrie's shoulder. "Darn right I did."

Carrie looked into his blue eyes feeling happy and complete. "I missed you, too, Jack."

Anna looked from Carrie to Jack. "I knew this was happening. I've seen it growing since the day the Pony Express began." She nodded her head happily. "You know, Jack, you have a bit of Seth Sutton in you. I can see why Carrie would love you."

Carrie looked at Anna with surprise and new understanding. This is how Anna must have felt about her father! This was love. I do love him, she thought. The world fell into place, as perfect as a world could be for a girl who had always wanted to be a boy and was suddenly, joyfully, glad to be a girl.

Epilogue

"I'll miss you, Anna," Carrie said, hugging Anna fiercely.

Anna was crying. "Oh, Carrie, I hate to leave when we've finally found our way to each other." She stood back and looked at Carrie, pride shining in her wet eyes. "Your father would have been so happy. You have become a most beautiful woman."

Carrie could see agreement reflected in Jack's eyes. He stood at her side as she said her good-byes to Anna. In honor of the occasion, Carrie was wearing the blue flowered dress that Anna had given her on her last birthday and her hair was pinned up precariously.

"Thank you, Anna," said Carrie. "Thank you for everything. I hope you have a safe trip home. Let us know how things are for you at home, what with the war and all. Please stay safe."

"I will, Carrie." Anna stepped over to Jack and hugged him quickly. "You take care of our girl, Jack."

Jack laughed. "I think my fiancée can take care of herself. I'm counting on her to take care of me." He hugged Anna back. "We'll be fine, Anna. You come visit us on the Sutton-Rising Ranch any time you get a hankering for some wide open spaces, all right?"

Anna laughed. "I'll be back for the wedding, don't forget that."

"That may not be for a while," Carrie reminded her.

The stagecoach driver politely interrupted them. "Time to go, ma'am." He held the coach door open and helped Anna into its interior. She leaned out the window and waved, tears still falling. "Good bye, good bye."

Carrie and Jack waved until the stage had passed around the corner and out of sight.

Jack looked at Carrie, raising his eyebrows. "You know, I don't see why you won't marry me now. Why wait?"

"I tried to explain this before. There's something I want to do first. I have to find Outlaw."

"Carrie, Outlaw's dead. They found him on the road, remember?"

"It was a mistake. It wasn't him. I don't think he's dead. You remember the dream I told you about, the one where I pictured your brothers exactly as they are? And I saw all the cattle? And then you brought that herd home, didn't you? Well, Outlaw was in that dream. He wasn't dead. He was there." Carrie started to get excited, thinking about Outlaw. "I'm going to find him, Jack Rising, and not you or anyone else is going to stop me. He's waiting for me. I can feel it."

Jack shook his head. "I guess if you've got to find out for sure, you've got to. But in the meantime we could get married, couldn't we?"

"When we get married, Jack, I want to ride off on our honeymoon on Outlaw's back, with you next to me on Flag. And it'll be that way, just you wait and see."

Jack laughed and caught Carrie up in a hug, spinning her around. "Life is never going to be dull as long as I'm with you, will it, Carrie?"

"Never, Jack, never."

Afterword

Riding On The Wind is a work of fiction set during actual historical events. Carrie Sutton did not exist. In all the research that I did I could not find a reference to a female pony rider. Until Carrie, there wasn't one.

Billy ("Buffalo Bill") Cody did live in those times, as did Captain Jack (Joe) Slade. If Cody was indeed a Pony Express rider, he would have been one of the youngest at fourteen. It is unlikely in spite of what he and others have written about his life, that he rode for the Express.

Jack (or Joe) Slade was a notorious Express division agent, who boasted of twenty-six murders. He died at the hands of vigilantes in Virginia City, Montana. Or so the story goes.

The Pony Express was a colorful and heroic footnote in America's and the postal services's histories. Many stories and the people involved can be found in the fine books listed in the bibliography.

Bibliography

Adams, Samuel Hopkins, *The Pony Express*. Illustrated by Lee J. Ames. New York: Random House, 1950.

Bloss, Roy S., *Pony Express, The Great Gamble*. Berkley, CA: Howell-North, 1959.

Bradley, Glenn D., *The Story of the Pony Express*. Chicago: A.C. McClurg & Company, 1913.

Chapman, Arthur, *The Pony Express*. New York: Putnam's, 1932.

Chapman, Arthur, *The Pony Express: The Record of a Romantic Adventure in Business*. New York and Chicago: A. L. Burt Company, 1932.

Cody, William F., *The Life and Adventures of "Buffalo Bill", an Autobiography*. Clinton, MA: The Colonial Press, 1927.

Driggs, HowardR., *The Pony Express Goes Through: An American Saga Told by Its Heroes*. Illustrated by William H. Jackson. New York: Frederick A. Stokes & Co.,1935.

Jensen, Lee, *The Pony Express*.New York: Grosset & Dunlap, 1955.

Nevin, David, *The Expressman*. New York: Time-Life Books, 1974.

Reinfeld, Fred, *Pony Express*. New York: MacMillan, 1966.

Root, Frank A., *The Overland Stage to California*. Topeka, KS: W. Y. Morgan. 1901.

Russel, Don, *The Lives and Legends of Buffalo Bill*. Norman, OK: University of Oklahoma Press, 1960.

Stein, R. Conrad, *The Story of the Pony Express*. Chicago: Children's Press, 1981.

Twain, Mark, *Roughing It*. Hartford, CT: American Publishing Co., 1872; New York: New American Library, 1962.

van der Linde, Laurel, *The Pony Express*. New York: Discovery Books, Maxwell MacMillan International, 1993.

Visscher, William Lightfoot, *A Thrilling and Truthful History of the Pony Express*. Skokie, IL: Rand McNally. 1908.

West, Tom, *Heroes on Horseback: The Story of the Pony Express*. New York: Four Winds Press, 1969.

Outlaws by Brix McDonald

Follow Carrie on her quest to find her stallion, Outlaw. Her determined search leads her to California's rugged High Sierras, where her encounter with the famous bandit Joaquín Murieta draws her into an adventure of a lifetime. *Outlaws* by Brix McDonald, more of the life and times of Carrie Sutton, coming soon from Avenue Publishing.

Brix McDonald has been an actress and playwright, a poet and children's theater director. And always a writer. She currently lives in Los Angeles with her husband, son, two dogs and four cats. Her lifelong love of books and horses has led her to write "Riding On The Wind". It is her first novel.